CONNECTED FOREVER

Written By: K.Y. Nelson

"Page turner, you keep the reader wanting more"

Ralph Duas

Cover Designed, Printed & Published by Valley Publishing
Co., a Division of Mays MultimediaDetroit, Michigan,
USA www.maysmedia.us Elizabeth Mays, Publisher

ISBN: 978-1-7349969-6-8

Printed in the United States of America.

About the Author

A little about me. My name is Kanisha Yolanda Nelson and I was born in Kalamazoo, Michigan a Borgess gorgeous baby on August 12, 1979. I was named by my grandmother and sister, but I look a lot like my mom; God rest her soul.

I have been blessed to have the talent to write and tell a story and I thank God for everything He has done in my life. I graduated from High school in Chicago, Ill, and continued on a couple of years later to receive my degree in Marketing and Advertising.

My mom always taught her children just to keep going, especially if it something you love to do. Don't let anything keep you from achieving your dreams. As long as you have faith, anything is possible. Life can take you on many rides that will test how strong the fight in you is

When I write I'm going into another world, a world of contentment! This is what writing means to me, it is my passion. I started out writing poetry when I was a teenager and decided to incorporate my life into expanding my experiences for the reader. I decided to challenge myself to complete my first Thriller/Suspense novel. This opened me up to a completely new experience which led me to writing my second novel with expectations of many more to come in the future.

Acknowledgement

As the years go by each road I have taken has led me on a different journey each time! Each time I came out at the end having learned a different lesson. Each time I came out mentally and physically stronger. I say all of that to say this, none of that would have been possible for me without having my faith in GOD, and not having any doubt that when I step out on faith everything will work out for the greater good.

I am more than grateful for my support system that continues to push me to accomplish my dreams with the talent I was blessed with to write and create a story to draw readers in.

I know my parents are looking down at me and are very proud of my accomplishments. I thank you dearly for instilling in me the strong values that I have. I love you!

I was raised with 6 siblings, and I am number 5 out of 7 in all. Every one of them in their own way inspires me to continue to keep going. They all shine in their own special way. I love each and every one of you tremendously!

A special thank you to my nieces and nephews. I want you all to continue to reach for your dreams. I am proud of you all and love each and every one of you unconditionally.

1 Michelle Sullivan

Finally, I had so much going for me. I was just promoted at the hotel to the night audit manager and was in a relationship with a wonderful man by the name of Jeremy Stone, who meant the world to me. Me? I was known to everyone as Michelle Sullivan. I stood 5'4, dark skinned, 140 pounds, and full of life, which is what everyone would always say about me. Even with all the good that was happening to me, I can never shake how I really am feeling. People didn't know that I held my real emotions in. I could not let the world see that what they saw as a happy life, was actually a distorted image.

On this particular day, I woke up to an eerie whisper in my ear, *I'm cold, it's so dark in here!*

Being startled out of my sleep, I sat up in bed noticing my nightie was soaking wet. I thought to myself, *what did I dream about? Why was I hearing voices?*

I looked at the time and realized I slept through my alarm, so I jumped out of bed and hopped in the shower, still feeling shaken by the voice that woke me up out of my sleep. I tried to take my mind off it by thinking about the fact that I was supposed to be meeting Jeremy for dinner later at one of the hottest spots in town after work.

When I got out of the shower, there was a missed call from Jeremy. He had left me a message saying he had to work late. Listening to his message made me think about when we first met at the Mocha Café, and all the events leading up until today. Before I knew it, I looked at my whole life standing before me! The memories flooded my brain. I recall this is my story from now until the end.

Moche Café was one of those spots you came to and everything else around you did not matter. It had two big picture windows in the front with a nook and bar stools so you could sit there, while you look out at the world. Or, you could sit at the round tables or booths decorated with little lamps holding tea light candles and enjoy the conversation of others. To top it all off, the subtle colors of deep wines and crèmes with historical pictures just made you relax. Now, what I like best about the café was the change of atmosphere in the morning. It was bustling with people from all walks of life; but after 5:00 pm, this was where most people came who worked downtown to unwind.

That day I had made plans with my best friend Kim to meet for dinner, so I went home after my shift and took a nap. I was so exhausted from working my night shift. It did not take me long before I dosed off after I sat down on the couch. As I slept, I started to hear the laughter of a little child. I was not disturbed by the laughter because I just assumed it was my subconscious playing tricks on me, especially since the TV was on when I fell asleep.

I woke up in a daze a few hours later by my cell phone ringing I struggled to open my eyes, not paying attention to the fact that the teddy bear I had gotten for Valentine's Day had been moved from the chair to the end of the couch. It was Kim calling to see if we were still on for dinner.

I ended up making it to the café before she did. I picked a booth close to the back of the Café, so I could see her when she walked in. I've known her since college. She is one of those friends who would tell you the truth no matter what, that is what I like about her. She is very determined. Kim is one of the top real estate agencies here in the city of Royal Oak, Michigan. She just has that kind of personality to connect with people. While I was waiting, my phone started to ring. It was Kim apologizing to let me know that she was not going to make it, she had to meet with a client. I thought to myself I will just go home, and relax in a nice bubble bath. But, I stayed and I'm glad I did.

I went ahead and ordered myself a glass of Merlot, while I made a decision on what I was going to have for dinner. Twenty minutes late, I was all set. I had my glass of Merlot and my main course, which was salmon over a bed of pilaf rice with French style green beans topped with sliced almonds. When I looked up, that's when I saw him.

Everything seemed to stop while Boney James was playing when he walked through the door There he stood, about 6'2" tall, dark skinned, beautiful complexion, and he had on a very nice charcoal grey tailored suit with a royal blue colored shirt, with a tie and shoes to match. They looked like high-quality Stacey Adams material. As he walked towards the back of the Café, I caught him take a glance at me and smile. I acknowledged back with eye contact paired with a shy smile to let him know that I was interested and was there alone. There was a glide to his walk when he brushed by my booth. His scent overwhelmed my senses. He was wearing Yves Saint Laurent cologne. It was intoxicating. Either I haven't been with a man in a while or he was just that handsome where I noticed every detail down to the fact that I could tell he works out by the sculpting of his muscles.

He went ahead and sat at the bar to order a drink. It looked like he was waiting on someone. As he sat with his back to me, I watched his body movement. I thought to myself, *Maybe he is already taken, and he is waiting for her to arrive*?

I finished up my meal and was beginning to take out my planner to look over my upcoming work week and any personal plans I may have had. Out of nowhere, a deep voice interrupted my thoughts.

"Excuse me miss, am I disturbing you? Do you mind if I sit here with you, my friend wasn't able to come down and celebrate with me tonight?" He said.

As my heart pounded, I somehow managed to keep my composure.

"You aren't disturbing me. Go ahead and sit down. What are you celebrating?" I said.

As he began to speak, I watched the movement of his lips wondering what they felt like. I thought to myself how glad I was I wore my ivory pencil legged skirt with my coral peplum top, because it accentuated my curves so well!

"I'm celebrating my promotion at Fusion Architecture. I am now the head architect of my department. My department handles the development of the new Buffalo Wild Wings. I forgot to introduce myself, my name is Jeremy Stone," he said.

"Well now isn't that interesting," I said with a coy laugh. "I do like their wings and congratulations on your promotion, Mr. Stone!"

"May I know your name?" He said with a smile.

"Yes, I'm sorry my name is Michelle Sullivan." I said.

"That's a beautiful name," he says with a little chuckle in his voice.

"May I ask what is so amusing?" I said.

"Oh, it's nothing," he replied. I found out later that he liked the sound of my name rolling off his tongue. He added, "so, what do you do for a living if you don't mind me asking?"

"No, I don't mind. I am the night audit manager at the Marriott Hotel."

"So, how do like the layout of area connecting to the Volt bar?" He said. *Wow, how does he know about the hotel*, I thought.

"I like the design of the area the open layout is very nice, but the only thing that kind of creeps me out is when I work nights it is a long distance to the ladies room. You have to walk around out of sight of the elevators and the front desk. It is very different at night though. There is no guest traffic, but you have the homeless from the downtown streets trying to sneak into the hotel and sleep."

"Well that could be partly my fault, because my company was involved in the remodel, so I apologize!" He put his hands up in a noncommittal gesture. "It is funny that I meet a woman who works up close and personal with my work. On the plus side, you get to see the sun set beautifully on that side of the building. Maybe, I could come and watch it with you someday?"

"Maybe," I said with a flirtatious smile.

"I don't mean to cut our conversation short, especially with such a beautiful woman, but I have a big day tomorrow. Our design project starts for the new Buffalo Wild Wings," he said.

"Oh, it is okay. I have to get home and prepare for my next workday as well."

"Do you mind if I walk you to your car?" He said. My heart fluttered.

"Actually, that is very nice of you to ask. Yes, it is okay." I said with a smile.

We headed towards my car and I hit the unlock button on my keys. Jeremy reached over to open the door and his body brushed against mine. As he waited patiently as I got in and put my purse in the passenger seat, he asked if I wanted his phone number so we could talk sometime.

"Yes, I will take your number!" I said trying to not sound too excited.

He then reached inside his jacket pocket and handed me his business card with a mischievous look on his face. "You have a good evening, Miss. Sullivan."

"Thank you, Mr. Stone. I will be in touch," I said as I watched him walk away.

In the privacy of my car, I said out loud "Mhmmm,

Mr. Stone I will definitely keep in touch." I knew I shouldn't get so wound up over this man, especially when I just met him!

On my drive home, I automatically started thinking how Jeremy is probably like all the rest of the jerks I have dated. But for me to move on, I need to forgive and forget. I mean he could be my knight and shining armor. I have not dated anyone seriously for the past year. Lately, I have dedicated myself to my job. Look where it has gotten me today! Maybe it is time for me to move on and share my growth with someone? Jeremy is established. I don't know if he has any kids, but I like children so that would not be a problem because I do want my own someday. See, there I go again jumping the gun and I haven't even called him on the phone. Let alone go on a second date, I don't think that was even considered a first date. I popped in one of my Mary J. Blidge CDs and tried to think maybe this time it could be different.

It was about 8:00 pm when I made it home. I headed upstairs to do my 45 minutes on the elliptical, and then run me some bath water. While the bath was filling up, I set out my uniform clothes for tomorrow night. Typically, this was my routine in the evening before my next night shift. As I slid down into my bath, I just told myself no matter how this goes with Jeremy, if it goes anywhere, I'm going to start over!

It was about 12:00 am when phone starting ringing, waking me from my sleep. Kim called me wanting to find out how my evening was. She is known for pulling long nights at the office.

"Hello, hey girl. How was your night?" She said.

"You would not believe what happened to me!" I exclaimed.

"What?" She said.

"I ordered my usual red wine and the Salmon meal. So just when I was finishing up, and about to go over my next week's agenda, a guy walked in! Jeremy Stone. He was tall, dark skinned, and very handsome. And when I say handsome, I mean handsome," I said.

"Did you say anything to him?" She asked.

"I didn't have too. He came to my booth and asked if he could sit down. He was celebrating his promotion at an Architecture firm."

"Girl! You got yourself an educated man!" Kim exclaimed over the phone.

"Slow down, Kim! You can't say that. We just had small conversation, but he did ask me if he could walk me to my car. Then, he gave me his phone number," I laughed into the phone.

"Yeah right! Michelle, I know that is not all. I have known you for 10 years, girl. You better spill it!" She said.

"Okay, I will tell you this when he reached over to open my door his body rubbed up against mine, and oh my goodness did he smell good. You know how it is when there is good looking man and he smells good too!" I said.

"Yeah girl, you better be ready to drop those panties," Kim said.

"You are so crazy," I said laughing. "I wonder sometimes how you keep your freakiness under wraps, Kim!"

"You know you are a freak too, don't even try it!" She said.

"I know, but listen it's getting late. I will tell you the rest of the story tomorrow over lunch, if you can make it?" I ask.

"I'll be there, girl. I will call you when I am on my way," she said. "All right, girl. Goodnight!"

"Goodnight, bye," I said.

After I got off the phone with Kim, I laid there holding Jeremy's card wondering again maybe, just maybe this could be it. I learned later that I should have listened to my gut when it came to Jeremy Stone.

The next morning, I was kind of dragging even though I did not have to be at work until this evening. I was so tired because my sleep was broken by Kim with her crazy self, but that's my girl. I threw on some cute workout gear and headed to Biggby's to get my regular, the big caramel chill. In the back of my head, I was hoping that I would run into Jeremy while I was out, but I didn't. I decided to go to the gym to take my mind off things, honestly to take my mind off Jeremy Stone.

As I was leaving the gym, my phone started to buzz. It was Kim.

"Hey girl, are you going to be able to make it for lunch?" She asked.

"Yeah, I just finished up at the gym and was about to head home and shower. I will meet you at Georgina's in about 45 minutes," I said

"Okay, girl. See you there."

When I arrived at Georgina's, Kim waiting there on the edge of her chair. You could see the anticipation on her face. She barely touched the food in front of her. I went ahead and ordered my lunch before Kim started to grill me about last night. As soon as I finished telling the waiter I wanted the chicken caesar salad, she started interrogating me.

"Michelle, have you been able to stop thinking about this mystery man? I bet not! You have to finish telling me about," she said.

"Well sort of, I was hoping that I saw him this morning when I ventured out while heading to the gym, but I didn't," I shrugged. "Anyway, what I didn't tell you about last night was that he helped design the new layout of the Marriott. He remarked how the sun sets so beautifully on my side of the building, and he asked if he could come see it." I said with a smile, just thinking about him being there made my stomach flip.

"What did you tell him, Michelle? You better have told him yes," she said.

"I told him maybe," I replied.

"Have you called him yet?" She asked.

"No, I haven't. But, I was thinking about inviting him to my birthday outing this weekend," I said.

"I think that would be a good idea, so I could tell you what I think about him. We don't need any more dead beats," she said.

"You are so right about that Kim. He seems so different. I just hope I am right!" I said.

"So, Friday you are off right?" She said.

"Yes, I requested it off." I said.

"Okay, cool. Let's go shopping for your sexy birthday dress," Kim said.

"Okay, Kim!" I laughed. "I will meet you at your office on Friday."

"All right, well I have to get back to work. See you Friday, girl," Kim said as she got up and left me to eat my salad alone.

2 Jeremy Stone

A few days later, my boy, Kyle called me up asking how my night out celebrating my promotion was. I played it off at first by just telling him it was dead in there for a Tuesday, making him sweat knowing I met a beautiful women.

"Aw, come on man! You're telling me there were no women in there that you noticed. Jeremy, you know it's about time you found someone you can share your success with man," he said.

"Yeah, I know. But it's hard to find the right one that will understand my hectic schedule and my hang ups," I said.

"What do you mean hang ups?" Kyle asked.

"Women want a lot from a man. I don't know if I am willing to sacrifice certain things to please her," I said.

"Sounds like you want your cake and eat it too, J. A women that is completely submissive," he said.

"That may make me sound like a jackass and cocky, but I do want that. I want free reign, man. But, I did meet a young lady on Tuesday. Her name is Michelle. She is very beautiful and smart. I think she might be the one that will follow me to the ends of the earth!" I said.

"You never know Jeremy she just might be the one to break you down, so when do I get to meet her?" Kyle said.

"Hold your horses, you will get to meet her eventually. Don't worry."

"Wait, come to think of it, it's funny you say Michelle, because I was with a Michelle last night," he said.

"What are you playing at, man? Was her name Michelle Sullivan?" I asked.

"Yeah that's her. And, man, that sista was a fine Coca-Cola shape, beautiful dark complexion, long black hair. She was hanging out with my girl, Kim," he said. "You are one lucky guy, what else did you find out about her?"

"I also found out that she works at the Marriott Hotel. The one we recently assisted on the remodel design. She is the night audit manager there," I said.

"Now, isn't that an interesting coincidence," he said.

"Yeah, maybe. Hey man listen, I will see you at the office so we can go over the blueprints around 11:00 am," I said.

"All right, man holla at you later!" Kyle said.

When I got to my office, I had voicemail from Michelle. She had the sexiest voice.

Hi Jeremy, its Michelle. I was calling to see if you were busy this evening? Give me a call if you are available. You can reach me at 313-264-8630. Bye.

I was kind of surprised she gave me a call after only two days. The way she said she would keep in touch made me think it would be longer than that. Miss Sullivan already has me wondering, and I like that in women. As much as I wanted to call her right back right then, I couldn't because I had to prepare the blueprints. I know Kyle will be happy to hear that she called when he gets here. He has been trying to set me up with someone for the longest. This could be it, but I'm not going to assume anymore. I could be wrong? Will she be able to handle who I really am? I am just really tired of women that look for what I can do for them and not what we can do for each other. I've had enough of that.

My phone rang, snapping me out of my thoughts about all the bad relationships I had been in. It was Eric and I already knew what he was going to say. His trifling girlfriend, Sheila plays with him more times than a Play station game, to be honest. I don't know how many times I have told him he needs to reevaluate his priorities.

"Hello, Jeremy Stone speaking."

"What's up, J. It's Eric!"

"Hey man what is going on, you alright?" I said.

"Yeah, I'm good man. Nothing much, the same old thing. Sheila is driving me nuts!" He said.

"Every time I talk to you it's the same thing. You talking about her messing with somebody else," I said.

"I think it's more than that this time, Jeremy. I know you don't do this anymore, but I need you to do some background work for me!" Eric exclaimed.

"What are you talking about Eric?" I replied.

"Man, she has just been canceling on me every time we have plans. I mean she answers when I call her, but she will just talk for a minute. And then, she'll say she would call me back," he said. "I can't figure out what's going on with her. She promised me that she is not messing around with anyone anymore."

"Eric, do you believe her?

"Yeah man, I have been with this girl too long not to believe her. We told each other after we were separated for a while that we were going to start over anew," Eric said.

"So, how long were guys separated?" I asked.

"For almost a year, she moved back to Michigan to live with her mom. Even then, she would still come down to visit me on and off. We would talk about the possibility of us getting back together. We would have romantic weekends," Eric said.

"I'm going to have to think about this. If I do it, I will call you with the details of what I will need," I said.

"Thanks, Jeremy. Man, you don't know what this means to me. I will owe you one."

"All right, man. I'll talk to you later." I hung up the phone.

Where is Kyle? He should be showing up pretty soon to go over the blueprints. Right as I thought that, my secretary buzzed through.

"Mr. Stone?" she said.

"Yes, Charlene. You have a Mr. Kyle Walters here to see you."

"Okay, thanks Charlene. You can send him in."

"Stone, you got those blueprints ready for me man?" Kyle said, as he walked into my office.

"Yeah, I got them. You are not going to believe this, guess who called me today?" I said.

"Who?" He said.

"Eric Mathews."

"Eric Mathews? Oh, that's the guy we worked with throughout college. What did he want? I didn't know you kept in contact with him." Kyle said.

"He wants me to do some research on Sheila Petty," I said reluctantly.

"Is he still with her?" he asked.

"Yeah, man. Now, she is telling him that she is not going to cheat on him anymore, she promised. Get this though, she cancels every time he plans something for them to do."

"Weren't they separated for a while?" Kyle asked.

"That's what he said. He also said that she would visit him, so they could have romantic weekends when she was living here in Michigan with her mom. So, you tell me what you think," I shrugged.

"It sounds like to me that she doesn't really want to be with him even though she promised," Kyle responded.

"I told him I would give him a call to let him know if I would do it or not, but I think I am just going to find out what is going on with Eric."

"Eric really needs to move on," he said.

"Yeah, I know. But, he is going to have to see for himself. It might not even be anything. He probably just needs reassurance. On a lighter note, guess who left me a message?" I smiled.

"It must have been Michelle," Kyle said.

"How do you know?" I said.

"For one you are standing there with a big smile on your face, you must really feel something for this girl, huh!" He laughed.

"Maybe!" I said.

"So, have you called her back? What did she say?"

"No, I haven't called her yet, but she just asked if I was busy this afternoon and left her number where she could be reached. I'll call her after we go through these blueprints," I said.

"It's just good to see you smile again. I thought me and the fellas were going to have to round up some money to get you a girl," Kyle said laughing.

"Man, whatever. let's get to work," I laughed.

Kyle is my boy. But, working with him can be a task sometimes. He likes to reminisce about the old times when we were in college. By the time we were done, it was

2:00 pm, and we started around 11:00 am.

"Okay, Kyle. We are all set. I will get the budget done for what we are working with for the project, and go over it before we start construction," I said.

I finally was able to call Michelle. As I dialed her number, I began to get nervous. This was weird for me, no women has ever made me feel this nervous. Typically, I was always the one making them nervous. The phone began to ring. On the third ring, I was going to hang up, but she picked up.

"Hello, hi Michelle. It's Jeremy!" I said.

"Oh, hi! How are you?" She replied.

"I am fine! I just got finished going over some things with my boy Kyle, he works here too. I figured you would be sleeping since you work nights," I said.

"I actually just woke up, I worked last night. I am off for the next few days, so are you busy this evening?" Michelle asked.

"No, my schedule is clear. What did you have in mind?" I said.

"Well, I know you mentioned in our last conversation that you would like to come and see the sunset with me at the hotel. Are you still open to that? Oh, I also wanted to invite you to my little birthday gathering I am having this weekend, too," she said.

Before I answered, a smile came across my face. "Sure, it would be nice to see something like that to relax me after the day I've had. And, I believe I can make it to your Birthday, too."

"Great, will 6:00 pm work for you tonight?" She asked.

"Yes, I will see you there," I smiled into the phone.

"Okay, see you then," Michelle said.

I sat back at my desk and started to imagine how this evening was going to go, but when you imagine the perfect thing it goes the opposite way. So, I'm going to just let it flow and see how it goes.

3 Sheila Petty

It was 2 o'clock in the morning when I heard someone banging on my apartment door in a panic. I got up with hesitation, and grabbed my metal bat that I kept tucked right next to my bed leaned up against my nightstand. I wasn't expecting anyone, so I was afraid of who could be on the other side of the door and why they would come to my apartment in the middle of the night.

I slowly walked to the door when I heard Kenny yell out, "SHEILA OPEN THE DAMN DOOR."

Hearing his voice stopped me right in my tracks! I opened the door making sure the chain was still latched before I did.

"Have you lost your mind? What the hell is wrong with you, showing up at my apartment this time of night? You know other people live here too," I whispered

"Whatever, girl. Let me in," Kenny grunted.

Kenny has always had a temper, which is one of the reasons why I had to let him go. This was a man that stood 6'4 and about 260 pounds. He pushed passed me busting the chain off the latch to come in.

I regret ever getting involved with him. For some reason, he thinks because we have some history I'm supposed to be in his life forever. I couldn't act irrational, because I didn't want to upset him anymore then he already was.

"Sheila, what you got to eat up in here?" He asked.

"Kenny?" I said with irritation, "why are you here?"

"You know I can't live without you. We have a deep connection, baby. Just let me show you I can do better," he said.

"Kenny, I told you it was over a long time ago. I have moved on!"

He immediately grabbed me by my neck, and said, "that's how it's going to be? All right, Sheila. I got you." His grip tightened around my neck.

As he had his hands around my neck, I stared into his eyes and saw an evil I never saw before. Right there, I knew that he had changed for the worse. Maybe he does need some actual help? I knew better than to fight him back. I didn't want him to tighten his grip around my neck. Although I knew he would never seriously harm me, but to be safe I told him he had to go stay at hotel. We could talk tomorrow. I haven't seen him in a couple of months, but I would talk to him. I know it was wrong to keep the line of communication open. I know Kenny has a temper, but I don't know what he is capable of now. He released his grip from around my neck and put his hands around my waist pulling me close to him.

"Come on, Sheila. You aren't gonna let me stay here?" He said.

I stretched my arms out trying to push him away as he continued to press, "it's not like I haven't had what you got Sheila!"

"Yeah well, that was then, and this is now. You have to go," I said standing close to my metal bat just in case he tried something again.

"Call me, when you get out of work!" Kenny said.

"Okay, Kenny," I sighed.

As soon as he walked out the door, I locked it and immediately ran to the window to make sure I saw him get in the car. This was all I needed, him showing up. Again, I couldn't help but to think this was my fault. I don't know how I can face Eric after I all I have put him through, especially when I promised that I would completely devote myself to him. He wants to start over with me, and if someone loves me that much, he deserves to be told the truth.

After my late-night disturbance, I was dragging the next day with only four hours of unsettling sleep. I went ahead and headed to work. As I walked to my car, I noticed

Kenny's car sitting at the corner of the building. I hurried around the back hoping he didn't see me. He has really got me paranoid. Looking back, that wasn't his car but one that looked just like his.

On my way upstairs to my apartment, I saw my girl Lisa. We've been friends for years. She moved to Michigan from Georgia a couple of months after I moved here.

"Hey, girl! Damn you look whooped, what were you doing last night?" She said with a smirk on her face.

"It's not even like that Lisa. Guess who came to my place at two in the morning," I said.

"OOOOOOH! I thought you said you were going to be faithful to Eric now," she said.

"Will you lower your voice?" I said to her with frustration. "I am faithful, and I told you it was not like that!" Lisa was starting to piss me off, but it wasn't her fault. It was, because of Kenny.

"Okay, well who showed up?" she said.

"It was Kenny." I looked down at my hands.

"What does his trifling ass want?" Lisa exclaimed.

"I don't know that's just it. He wants me to call him after I get off work. For a second, I thought I saw his car around the corner," I said.

"So, where did he stay last night?" She said.

"I told him he had to go stay at a hotel. When I told him it was over a long time ago and that I have moved on, he grabbed me around my neck," I said.

"Well do you want me to call the police, I don't want to see anything happen to you!" Lisa said.

"No, I don't want any more problems. Besides I saw something else in his eyes last night that I never saw before in Kenny, and honestly it scared me." I shuttered at the memory.

"Sheila, you know I got your back. Don't ever think I won't be here for you, we have been friends too long for me not to," Lisa said.

"I know you are, and I appreciate you for that. I'm going to see what he wants after work, and I will definitely let you know what's up!" I said.

"Sheila listen, when you meet up with Kenny later, do me a favor go to the bathroom and text me to let me know where you are at with him in case you need me to roll through. Even better I can sit in disguise, because he is known to act stupid even in a public place," she said.

"I appreciate that Lisa, but I will be fine. Let's just

try to make it through the day," I sighed.

After we had our morning meetings with Kimberly, our Accounting Supervisor, and a colleague of mine, Eric called me to see how my day was going.

"Hey sweetie, how is your day going today?"

"I guess everything is going okay," I sighed.

"What do you mean you guess, what's wrong?" He asked.

"I am swamped with this new project, and I have to work through lunch," I said.

"Aww honey, that's too bad! I wanted to come and treat you to a nice romantic lunch," he said.

"Oh, baby. That is so sweet of you, I'm sorry," I said.

"Sheila, you don't have to be sorry. I can bring it to you," he said.

"NO, NO, NO," I said too quickly. "You don't have to go through all of that."

"You sure you are all right, Sheila?" Eric said with curiosity.

"Yeah, I'm fine. I will call you after I get off work

today," I said.

"Okay baby." I could hear the disappointment in his voice.

"I got to go babe, bye."

I didn't want to rush him off the phone, but I could not risk Kenny seeing Eric. I had no idea if he followed me or not! Any other day seemed to drag, but today flew by. It was 5:00 pm before I knew it.

I couldn't even get my coat on good before Kenny started blowing up my phone.

"Hello, what's up Kenny?"

"I know you weren't going to try and skip out of here without calling me first!" He exclaimed.

"Damn, Kenny! You didn't give me a chance to call you either, did you?" I said.

"Don't get smart with me, Sheila. Where do you want me to meet you at?" He said.

"Come up to the third floor of the parking garage of my work building. We can talk here, I'm in the tan Nissan Altima," I said.

As I waited for him to make it up here, I thought *what the hell am I doing*? I should have met him in a place where there were more people around. I know if I don't talk to him, he is just going to keep harassing me. And, who says for sure after I talk with him that he is just going to go away. When I saw him turning the corner I got out of the car and motioned to him to let him know he could park here next to mine.

He rolled down his window and said, "why don't you come and sit in the car with me, Sheila."

If I know Kenny like I think I know Kenny, he still carries that Ruger P89 Semi-Automatic Handgun 9mm Blue Steel under his driver seat. But, that isn't going to stop me from standing my ground.

"No, I will pass on that invitation. You can get out and stand right here with me," I said. I couldn't show him that I was nervous, especially after the way he choked me last night. He feeds off that type of energy!

"So, how have you been doing Sheila? You have really come up from driving that old beat up escort back in the day to driving a Nissan Altima." He nodded appreciatively.

"CUT THAT CRAP KENNY, WHAT DO YOU WANT? I DON'T HAVE ALL NIGHT FOR THE SMALL TALK," I said.

He stepped closer to me mushing his face up against

mine, he whispered in my ear, "I know one thing Sheila you better calm your ass down. I know you didn't forget that fast what happened last night."

"Just because you feel like that is what a man is supposed to act like, Kenny. I'm sorry, but you are about to have a rude awakening. I am not afraid of your punk ass. Never have been, and never will be."

He looked at me and gave me a devilish smirk and said, "now, that is what I'm talking about. You know I like it when you get like that. Baby, you know we are meant for each other. You remember when we used to drive up to Bell Isle and make love in my car? I would take you, and the baby shopping—"

I cut him off, "I told you that day is dead and gone. You couldn't even respect me enough to take me away for the weekend. I guess I was a quick screw. And, just because you bought me and my son a few things that doesn't make it okay for all of the verbal abuse, drug dealing, and the cheating."

"Sheila, don't be a bitch. One: you won't even let me see my son. Two: don't act like you weren't all up in my bed when you and whoever this nigga is were separated. Oh and don't act like I didn't know you were telling him that you were staying with your nana when you were coming down here to look for a place," he said

35

with a smirk. "You and I have known each other for five years. You had Micah at 22 years old. I know you haven't changed in the past five years. Now, you won't even let me get close to you anymore."

"Kenny, true we have kept in touch and I messed around with you when I was separated from the man I'm with now, but my heart is here with him now. So, all I can tell you is to move on. My son doesn't need anyone like you in his life," I said.

I could see the hurt in his face, he paused for a moment and raised his hand to me like he was going to knock me to the ground, and just as he did a car pulled through the parking garage, Kenny quickly put his hand down and said, "this is not the last you're going to see of me."

He got in his black Impala and proceeded to drive off. I saw then, as well as last night, Kenny has really changed for the worse. I pray that he will change.

4 Kim Shavers

"Hey, Baby. Guess what?" I said.

"What's up, Kim?" Kyle asked.

"I just sold that $530,000 house in Grosse Pointe Farms. You know the four bedroom house with the three bathrooms. It has the cathedral ceilings, fireplace, skylights, and the pool in back," I said excitingly.

"Are you kidding me, you been trying to sell that house for at least a month now," he said.

"I know, but I was patient and the right family came along. The husband is a Dentist with his own practice, and the wife is a partner at Michaels and West law firm," I said.

"So, Mr. Walters do you want to celebrate with me tonight?

"Of course, baby. You know I like it when you call me Mr. Walters. I will see you around 8:00 pm," he said.

"Okay. I will be waiting for you with the candles lit, chocolate covered strawberries, and Champagne," I said with a smile.

"Your making me wish it was 8:00 already, Miss. Shavers." He laughed into the phone.

"Well, now you know what you have to look

forward to. I've got to let you go, sweetie. I have another call coming through," I said.

"Okay. Love you, bye!" Kyle said.

"Kim Shavers speaking," I said.

"Hey girl, it's Michelle."

"Hey, what's up?" I said.

"You remember how I called Jeremy and left him a message?"

"Yeah, I remember. Why? He didn't call you back?" I said.

"No! That's not it. He did call me back. I invited him over to the Marriott to watch the sunset with me on my day off." I could hear the excitement in her voice.

"Gone, Miss. You better behave," I said.

"Kim, it has been so long since I have even entertained a man!"

"Michelle just be yourself. It's like riding a bike, you won't forget how to do anything when it comes to a man. I do know this though, take it slow and things will fall right into place."

"Thanks, Kim! this is another reason why you are

my girl." Michelle laughed into the phone. "Do you have any big plans for the evening?"

"Yes! I sold that big house I have been trying to sell for at least a month. Kyle and I are going to celebrate at my house tonight." I smiled.

"Wow, congratulations! I am so happy for you. I'm going to have to treat you to dinner tomorrow when we go shopping for my birthday dress."

"Thank you! What time is Jeremy supposed to be meeting you at the Marriott?" I asked.

"At 6:00, I only have an hour before he gets here," she said.

"All right, girl. Well you better let me know how everything goes," I said.

"I will. Enjoy your evening as well. Talk to you later, bye."

I really hope everything goes well for her this evening. It's about time she finds someone that will love Michelle inside and out. I went ahead and finished up some paperwork before I headed out to set up things at my house before Kyle came over. I had to stop at the store to pick up some fresh strawberries, white and pink rose petals, and chocolate. I already had the champagne at home. By the time I finished up the paperwork and went to the grocery store it was 6:30 pm. I had to have everything all set by the time Kyle gets here, because I know he is going to be on time. He is a stickler for that.

When I made it home, the first thing I did was put in an Alicia Keys CD, a Maxwell CD, and an Old School mix CD, and set it to a program of the songs I wanted to be played. I whipped us up a quick meal of shrimp fettuccini alfredo and some garlic bread. Then, I began to melt the chocolate for the strawberries while the chocolate was simmering over a low fire. I placed the champagne in the freezer so it would be chilled when I served dinner. After I dipped the strawberries, I sat them in the fridge to cool down, and began to set the mood for each room.

In the dining room, I set up two of my oval shaped bowls in the middle of the table filled them with a little water to place some floating candles inside. When I finished there, I headed upstairs to my master bathroom to set the scene for a hot bath in my Jacuzzi tub afterwards. I set out the lavender bath oil, bath salt, and bubble bath for relaxation. I placed the rose petals around the top of the tub, alternating colors, as well as on the floor leading from the entrance of my master bedroom to the bathroom. Everything was in place like I had planned, all I needed to do was get dressed. I put on my black dress that was form fitting, that had the cow neck in the front with my strapless black lace bra and panty set under it. To complete my outfit,

I selected my 4 inch stiletto opened-toe shoes. All I needed to do now was my hair and touch up my make-up. I pinned up my hair with some swoop bangs down in the front with a tri-pendent necklace, and studded earrings to match.

The doorbell rang just as I put on the last touches to my make-up, it was 8:00 pm. Kyle was right on time. Kyle was 6ft with a caramel complexion. He must have gone home to change because he had on his gray slacks, Zengara shoes, and a black Polo shirt with Perry Ellis's 360° cologne.

"Oh, Baby. You look so damn good," he said as he gave me a huge hug.

"Thank you. You don't look too bad yourself, Mr. Walters," I said with a smile.

"So, what smells so good?" He asked.

I grabbed his hand and led him into the dining room, "you sit here while I prepare your plate."

Before I walked away, I gave him a sensual kiss on the lips. I had Alicia Keys, "The diary" playing as I brought in our dinner on square shaped plates with oriental designs on them.

"This looks so good! Shrimp fettuccini Alfredo, you made this from scratch?" Kyle said.

"Yes, I just wanted to do something special for you. This is just the start of it, so just continue to relax while I grab the champagne," I said. I poured our drinks, we held hands and said prayer before we began to eat.

"I am so glad you were able to make it, Kyle. I know you and I have been busy with work, but we have been together for two years and you're an amazing man. I love you!" I exclaimed.

"I don't know what to say Kim," he said.

"Well, I was hoping for a better answer than that," I sighed.

"No! It's not that baby! It's just that I have been feeling the same way too. I'm relieved that I am not the only one feeling this way in our relationship. I love you too, Kim." He said with a broad grin.

I smiled at him as he held my hand. I finally found someone who is willing to give me as much as I give for them. I know this was not the first time I have expressed my feeling towards him, but this moment seemed like the first time for some reason.

As I snapped out of a quick daydream, I asked him how he was enjoying his meal. His answer matched what I was thinking, because it was almost gone.

"Are you going to be able to come to Michelle's

birthday party with me Saturday?" I asked.

"Yeah, I don't see why not. I hope she brings this new guy she met at the Mocha Café."

"Is his name Jeremy Stone by any chance?" He laughed.

"How do you know him?" I was shocked.

"He was my college buddy and we work together," he said.

It all made sense now, it was his friend, J from work he talked about that I never met. "You didn't think to mention this to me on the phone earlier?" I asked.

"I'm sorry I forgot! He was telling me about her, and I told him that she was friends with you. It is a small world huh? Jeremy is a great guy, although he has his hang ups. I hope they hit it off," Kyle said.

"I do too baby," I said as I got up to sit on his lap, overlooking him saying that Jeremy has had some hang ups. I gave him a couple of soft kisses on his neck as I asked, "are you ready for dessert?"

"Can I have seconds if I like it?" He smirked.

I let out a little laugh and smiled as I said, "I'll meet you upstairs in the master bathroom."

He came up to me pulled me close and whispered in my ear, "don't take too long."

When I got upstairs, he was standing next to the Jacuzzi waiting on me with nothing on except his Jockey boxer briefs displaying his sexy athletic body, and his bulging package that I couldn't wait to caress. He had his clothes neatly folded on the bench next to the tub. I had the chocolate covered strawberries in my left hand, and the champagne and two glasses in the other.

Kyle walked up close to me and kissed me passionately while he grabbed the strawberries out of my hand, saying, "let me help you with the dessert."

He sat the strawberries down at head of the tub along with the champagne. Then, he proceeded to undress me by sitting me down, unbuckling my heels one by one. He laid me back on the chair and pulled my body forward sliding my panties down to the floor. He placed my legs on his shoulders, while he was on his knees as he proceeded to taste me flicking his tongue back and forth. I felt the first sensual kiss on my private lips. I let out a soft moan of ecstasy as I ran my fingers across the top of his head. I could feel his hands squeezing my thighs pulling me closer into him. He continued to move his tongue from a soft circular rotation to an exotic cyclone. I closed my eyes as my body began to quiver overflowing with my love for Kyle.

He gave me playful bites on the inside of my thigh before he stood me up and lifted my dress over my body as my back was facing him. I had Goosebumps all over my body as I felt his hand stroke down the middle of my back while he unhooked my bra. It was not enough, he tasted my forbidden places he turned me around and picked me up bracing my back against the wall I clinched his back as his throbbing dick slid inside me, feeling every inch. My body responded to the curve of his dick as we went from the wall to up against my dresser.

By this time Maxwell's CD was playing, he flipped me over grabbed my hair and teased me with the tip of his dick before he stroked me all the way over. I couldn't let Kyle have all the fun, so I pulled away led him to the bed laid him down on his back and took all his eight inches into my mouth. I took my tongue and twist it around the tip, before I deep throated Kyle. I did not know his voice could go as high as it did, I went up and down on his pulsating dick before he exploded in my mouth.

We eventually made it into the tub, where Kyle said to me, "Kim, let me help you down into the tub. I want you to lie back, I'll massage your feet. And then, I'm going to massage your shoulders, gently wash your body, and dry you off."

The whole time we were in the tub, we talked about our future plans together. After he wiped me down. He led

me to my bed and pulled out the body oil. He asked me to
light some extra candles and lie on my stomach. He rubbed
me down from head to toe. As my body drifted further into
relaxation, I did not think the night was going to end like
this.

5 Michelle Sullivan

It was almost 6:00 pm. I wore my yellow halter dress with my blue jean crop jacket. The anticipation was killing me. When Jeremy arrived, I began to get that funny feeling all over, like the one you get in high school when you had to stand up in front of the class to introduce yourself. There were glass doors leading to the outside bar lounge where they had a circular sofa surrounding an outdoor fire pit. I could see him walking down the hallway, and all I could think was *damn, he looked like he was a model stepping out of GQ a magazine*. I couldn't let my thoughts be expressed on my face.

This time he was dressed down. He had on dark colored blue jeans and a nice blue polo shirt with all black running shoes. He began to smile as he got closer and saw the outdoor lounge area with the fire pit.

"Hi Jeremy, you look nice this evening," I said with a smile.

"Well thank you, Michelle. I have to say you are one of the sexiest Night Audit Managers I have ever seen in all of Michigan."

"Thank you." I had to stop myself from blushing. "So, how does it feel to be looking at the finished product of your amazing work?"

"I haven't seen it up close and personal since it was completed, I have been very busy at work. But, I must say the decorator for the Volt bar did a great job. Wow, I'm really impressed." He looked around admiringly.

"So, is this what you imagined? Would this have been something you would have chosen for the outdoor lounge?" I asked.

"Actually, it is very close to what I would have chosen. I do know a thing or two about decorating. You should see my house," he said as he walked closer to me.

He put his hand on my waist looked directly into my eyes and smiled. It wasn't a mischievous smile or a nervous smile, this smile showed confidence in him. He led me over to a chase lounge for two that was covered by a private tent facing the sunset. He sat down first and took off his shoes. I looked at him and thought, *is this real or is it one of my dreams that have finally come true*. Jeremy grabbed my hand and turned me around to sit in between his legs as hands gently went down my leg to remove my shoes as well. All the while my head was lying on his chest, I could smell his cologne and feel his muscle tone. With his arms wrapped around me, he grabbed my throw blanket that I brought just in case it got chilly and put it over us. I never felt so secure and comfortable with anybody in my life. We laid there waiting for the sunset and talked about our lives, excluding our careers. The questions kept coming to me, and he had no problem answering. I did the same for him when he asked me questions. Down to what our middle names were!

"I can tell you like subtle colors. It seems that every so often, you would where a very daring color like red, which I might add you would look very beautiful in," Jeremy said.

"You're good, I like that you pay attention to detail." I smiled at him.

"Well, when it comes to someone like you. I will always be on my P's and Q's," he said.

"That's sweet, Jeremy. Since we are asking questions, what type of women are you used too?" I asked.

"Not any women like you."

"I guess I could take that as a compliment," I said with some curiosity.

"It's like this: since college, you know you date and everything, but when all the people you tend date want to see what they can get out of you and not the relationship. It gets old you know? I'm kind of old school when it comes to the women I would want to be with. This would go on even after I got out of college, so I stopped dating for a while. I dove into my work, got that promotion, and then I ended up meeting you, which is another good accomplishment in my life so far," he said.

"You know what I think. We should have met back then so we could have hooked my dead-beat ex-boyfriends up with your gold-digging ex-girlfriends," I said.

"That would have been nice," he said laughing, as he held me tighter. "Ok, Michelle I have the most important thing to ask, can you cook?"

"Yes! I can boil water," I said seriously.

He paused, and said, "oh! That's okay, I can cook. I could teach you a few things."

I couldn't hold it in anymore I started to laugh. "Oh, you think I can't teach you anything. You are just going to have to wait and see on our next date!"

"No, No, No, it's not that I can't cook. I was messing with you. I can cook. I love to cook, it's something I really enjoy," I said.

"Well, well, well, we are just going to have a cook off then. We can invite some friends over and they will be the judges," Jeremy said.

I looked up at him right into his dark brown eyes, and said "okay, you are on!"

The sun could not have set at a more perfect time,

because he caressed the side of face, and said, "I accept your challenge."

He leaned down and gave me the most romantic kiss that took my breath away. After the sun was completely set, the lounge was lit up by streetlights. I was surprised when he asked me if it was ok if he stayed a little while, because he enjoyed having me in his arms.

"Yes, of course it is fine. I'm enjoying this too."

It was like we were out here by ourselves, even though we weren't. The satellite radio started to play on the lounge and the music was old skool.

"Are you into old skool," I asked him. I got up and started to sway my hips flirtatiously to the music and he watched me with excitement in his eyes.

"Girl! Are you kidding me? I may only be 28, but I get down with some Marvin Gaye. And, don't get me started on the Temptations! Do you want me to keep going? Or are you going to come back over here and let me hold you some more," he said.

This night was going better than I expected I walked back over, and Jeremy pulled me on top of him, and began to kiss me. I could feel the strength of his hands around my waist, down to my thighs, back up to squeezing butt. When you get involved with a man who is built like Jeremy, you know he has some strong hands. I almost lost myself in his touch, but he remained a gentleman and did not try to go any further. Part of me was glad that he was a gentleman, but the naughty part of me was saying, OH YES BABY, YOU KNOW WHAT YOUR DOING!

I continued to lie on his chest. When we finished listening to the old school slow jams, we called it a night. Once again, he made sure I made it to my car safely, and then kissed me goodnight, and said, "I will give you a call."

"Okay, I will talk to you soon."

His car was not parked that far so I waited for him to get in before I drove off.

6 Eric Mathews

"This is Jeremy Stone. Leave a message after the beep."

"Hey Jeremy, man. It's Eric, holla at me when you get this message," I said.

As I was driving, I couldn't stop thinking about Shelia. I can't believe she blows me off every time I try to do something nice for her. She always has some kind of excuse. I'm really starting to think she is still messing around. I wonder why I ever thought about starting over with her and making a future. I must have been crazy!

After Sheila cancelled on me, I decided to go somewhere close downtown to sit and grab a sandwich before I had to go back to the bank. As I was sitting there, I saw Lisa, Shelia's friend walk by. I motioned her over to sit with me during lunch. Now, Sheila was my fine ass caramel beauty, but the way things have been going with Shelia and the back and forth about her feelings. Part of me wants to just let it go, but I feel like I need some answers first. I love my girl. Lisa wasn't Sheila, but Lisa was looking kind of good. She was stacked, brown skinned, short hair, hazel eyes, and stood about 5'5". I had heard some things about her from Sheila that Lisa can't keep her mouth shut. So, if I play my cards right, I can juice her for all I need to know.

"Hey Eric, how ironic I run into you? I was just

with your girl at work before I stepped out for lunch," Lisa said.

"Yeah, my baby works hard. She had to miss lunch with me today," I said.

"I know, Sheila keeps everything under control. I have always wondered how she controls her emotions so well. No one could ever tell if she has a lot of things going on in her life," she said.

"What do you mean by that Lisa? Did she tell you something that is going with her, because she has been kind of distant with me? I mean she has a lot going at work, but I have a feeling it could be something else," I said.

I was wondering if me talking about this would get Lisa to start talking. I was right, because no sooner than that she put her hand on my knee looked me straight in the eye, slightly biting her bottom lip.

"You know what, Eric? You're a great guy and I really think you should start looking out for yourself. I have known Sheila for some years now, and she is known to be selfish when it comes to the men. I mean the man in her life," she said.

"I thought you and Sheila were tight, Lisa!"

"We are, but I'm just telling you like it is. I am telling you that I don't like what I see. You are in pain. You care so much about someone who doesn't want to give her all to you," Lisa said.

Sheila was not lying when she told me about Lisa. She did not waste any time putting it out there that she was attracted to me. I can tell, but it was all a part of my plan! Lisa stood up and leaned towards me making sure her cleavage was showing and whispered, "If you need someone to talk to or a late night companion, I am here," she said as she slipped her business card in my front jacket pocket.

Damn, this girl is so attractive. She is my bait now. By the way she was acting, Lisa wasn't going to say anything about this lunch to Sheila. She was too busy trying to make Shelia look bad. I need to get in contact with Jeremy again, so I could have him get started in on Sheila. The way Lisa was acting she knows something I don't. This girl is slick. She only told me what she wanted me to know for the time being, so I would have to call her!

I called Sheila after I got off work around 6:30 pm to see how the rest of her day went.

"Hey Baby, how did the rest of your day go? Were you able to get everything finished with your project that you needed to get done?" I asked.

"Hey, sweetie! The rest of my day went okay. I'm just exhausted, I didn't get much sleep last night." She sighed into the phone.

"Oh!" I said with some hesitation and curiosity. "Why were you up so late?"

"I had to type up the accounting reports for the different departments in the building," she said. It sounded like a lie to me, but I ignored my gut.

"Well, it sounds like someone needs to be treated to the spa this evening. Are you up for it?" I asked.

"Yes, that would be just what I need," she said.

"Okay, see you around 7:30?" I asked.

"Sounds good, I will be ready then."

It was 7:30 pm. I rang the doorbell. When she opened the door to let me in, I went in for a hug and a kiss. Her face scrunched up, like kid would do when they are being kissed by a parent.

"Hello to you too Eric, can I breath?" She asked.

"Oh, I'm sorry, baby. I thought I might get you in the mood before the hot tub at the spa!" I said.

"Baby, I am not really in the mood for that right now," Shelia said. I stepped back and looked at her suspiciously.

"Why are looking at me like that Eric?" I asked.

I couldn't take it anymore, I could feel my emotions take over, "COME ON SHEILA, YOU KNOW I HAVE BEEN THROUGH A LOT OF BULL CRAP WITH YOU!"

"Eric, why are yelling? I told you I was exhausted. You know what? I think you should just leave. I don't have time for your paranoia, especially when I told you that I only want to be with you," she said.

"I'm sorry, I'm sorry," my shoulders dropped, I had to let go of my anger. "I told you that I was going to treat you to a relaxing evening, and that's what I'm going to do. If you want me to go home after that, I will."

When we arrived there, I hurried and jumped out of the car to open Shelia's door. I got us the outside hot tub where you could look up at the stars for two hours. It was so nice there was a fireplace adjacent from the hot tub, a garden bench, statues, and beautiful plants surrounding the hot tub. We were able to set the radio to whatever station we wanted, so I put jazz on for Shelia, since it was her favorite. When I stepped down into the water, my body immediately felt stress free.

Why does it always seem like when you're enjoying yourself time flies, before we knew it the two hours were up! I had my overnight bag ready just in case Shelia changed her mind about me staying at her place, but she told me she would rather stay with me tonight at my place. I wasn't going to object.

I took her home to get some clothes for the next day, and when we got there I noticed that the light was blinking on her answering machine. I sat down on the coach. I was surprised when she pressed play, "you have one new message left at 8:00 pm: Hey girl, it's Lisa listen I was just calling to see how your situation went, because you haven't called like you said you would, give me a call bye!"

The conversation with Lisa rang through my mind. But, what situation was she talking about? I had to ask.

"What was she talking about?" I asked.

"Oh, nothing. It's a family situation that's all."

"Is your mom okay?" I asked.

"Yeah, she is fine!" she said. "Are you ready to go? It's getting kind of late and I need some rest."

"Yeah, give me your bag. I will carry it down to the car," I said.

When we arrived at my house, we both put our night clothes on. I slept in my boxers. She put on a spaghetti strap camisole and some lace boy cut panties. I held her close and I kissed her on her neck and said goodnight.

7   *Kyle Walters*

"Hey J, its Kyle give me a call when you get this. You won't believe the night I had."

I was high off Kim today. Man, I love that girl. I headed into the office. I have to focus. I can't be sidetracked all day looking at Kim's picture on my desk. As soon as I got into the office, my phone rang.

"Hello, Kyle Walters speaking."

"Hey man, it's Jeremy. What's going on?"

"Hey man! Kim and I had an amazing night!"

"Really?" Jeremy asked. "Well I can tell you this before you get started in on any details, you weren't the only one."

"What you mean?" I asked.

"I hung out with Michelle last night. That girl is amazing. Nothing happened, but she is just that amazing where it didn't have to turn out that way," he said. "Now it's your turn to spill it. It must have been good if you of all people called me so early."

"Okay, check this out. Kim calls me up letting me know she sold a house that she has been trying to sell for the last couple of months." I paused.

"This must have been some house if you're this excited!" Jeremy said.

"Yeah, I was! It was a really big deal for Kim. It was a $530,000 house," I said.

"Damn man, that is great!"

"So, she tells me to meet her at her house yesterday. She had dinner made, chocolate covered strawberries, and rose pedals surrounding her Jacuzzi tub. She went all out," I said.

"You going to mess around and get her pregnant. I'm going to be some little boy's or girl's uncle," he said.

"That is shocking you say that knowing you don't want any of your own," I laughed.

"True, Michelle would have to go if she came at me with the whole having babies conversation. Other than that, sounds like you're on cloud nine right now my brutha."

"I am." I laughed, adding, "enough about me, tell me about your evening with Michelle."

"We met at the Marriott where she works to watch the sunset, because she had said it was beautiful. The outdoor lounge at the Volt bar was a sight to see. You have to take Kim there one day. There is an outdoor fire pit and private chase lounges covered with tents. It was so nice, man. Anyway, we chatted a little bit and I relaxed on the chase lounge Things got a little intense when the bar turned on some old school and the sun was setting, but I remained a gentleman and I'm glad we had the privacy of the tent." He laughed into the phone.

"I know you are a gentleman, J."

"Yeah, a real gentleman," he sarcastically said.

"Man, whatever. You think you are funny, don't you?" I asked.

"The night ended up with me walking her to her car and kissing her goodnight," he said.

"It sounds like we have a winner with this one," I said.

"Yeah, man. I like her. Let's just hope things stay that way," he said.

"I know, because you have had some crazy ones in the past."

"So, you think you're going to get up with her this weekend?" I asked.

"Actually, she invited me to her birthday gathering she is having this weekend. Since your lady is real cool with her, maybe we can do double date with you and Kim sometimes? Did you know about the party?" He asked.

"No, but I'm sure Kim is going to mention it. I'll go with her," I said.

"All right, man."

"Let me know if you want to meet up before the party, because I don't think I have to come your way to look at any blueprints today," I said.

"No, you don't. I will holla at you later!"

"Hey, wait! Has Eric said anything else to you about that Sheila situation?" I asked.

"No, but I'm sure I will hear from him before the weekend is up. I'll keep you posted man, but I will talk with you later," Jeremey said.

"A'ight, J. Talk to you later!" I said.

I thought to myself how long I have known my boy, Jeremy. Him talking about Michelle was starting to stir up memories of his past relationships. It brought back memories of a relationship he had junior year in college that was alarming to me. Her name was Crystal Stevenson and she was a pharmacy major. They met in his calculus class that semester. It all started out very innocent with them going to group study sessions together. The next thing you know those sessions turned into them studying in either his dorm room or hers. Things were going well with him and Crystal, until the night of the storm. Jeremy came banging on my dorm room door. I will never forget that night. I really hope that the Jeremy I saw that night doesn't resurface again in this new relationship with Michelle.

I had just finished writing my Econ paper, the storm was kicking up and the lightning was rolling across the sky. I stood up to look out the window at the storm when Jeremy begin to frantically knock on my door. Who the hell is banging on my door at this time of night and why would they be out in this type of weather? When I looked through the peep hole, I saw it was Jeremy and his clothes were soaking wet. He was out of breath gasping for air when I opened the door. Did he run here from his dorm?

I immediately saw the fear in his eyes. A look I will never forget seeing on my friend's face.

"J, what the hell is going on?" I asked.

Frantically he started to speak, and said, "Kyle, man. I think I fucked up. I need your help."

I didn't know what to expect when I invited him in, he rushed past me and started to pace back and forth mumbling what am I going to do repeatedly, before he sat down on the bed holding his head in the palm of his hands. I sat down cautiously on the bed directly across from him and asked him , "J, what's up man?" Whatever happened, it's going to be okay!"

He began to slowly speak about the events that unfolded that night with his head still hanging low in disappointment.

"I don't know what to do, man…"

I slowly stood up with hesitation and I asked, "Jeremy, where is Crystal?"

I was frozen waiting for his lips to move! In my head, I was praying that my good friend who was sitting before me didn't do anything terrible to that girl.

He finally looked up at me and said, "I don't know if she is going to be okay! I didn't mean to push her. I didn't mean to hit her that hard… I just lost it when she kept forcing the subject."

I couldn't do anything but sit and listen in disbelief as he continued to speak, and you could hear it in his voice how scared he was that he thought he had harmed her badly.

"She came over around 7:00 pm because she wanted to talk, and I didn't think anything of it because we had a disagreement earlier about her thinking that I had become distant lately. When she got there, I can tell that she had been crying and there was something else bothering her. I invited her in. I went and sat down beside her to wrap my arms around her to comfort her and to ask her what was wrong. I noticed she was fidgeting nervously when she mumbled the words, I'm pregnant without even looking at me." He shuddered.

"Pulling away from my arms being wrapped around her, she scooted back and looked at me responding with the same irritation in her voice saying, 'I'm pregnant Jeremy.' Her hands were placed crossed on my knee expressing calmness, but I felt like she was trying to trap me she knew the basis of our relationship and her purpose. I pushed her hands away in anger and stood up over her. My anger was consuming me. I raised my voice saying, 'how could you be so careless, you already know I'm not trying to be locked down!' The storm began to get louder as she rose up off the bed getting in my face yelling back at me saying, 'you are not going to treat me like I don't matter! You feel like you can use my body whenever you want for your sexual needs?' All I could see was red, the rage tinted my vision. I gripped her arms tightly pushing her up against the wall. She didn't realize that is all she is good for. I told her that. When I said that it enraged her even more. She broke loose from my grip, slapping me across my face, crying and yelling at the same time saying she was keeping the child." He took a deep breath.

"I wrapped my hands around her neck shaking her frantically like a rag doll out of anger I threw her to the floor. I continued to rant at her saying you know you had a reputation before we got together not paying attention to the fact that she hit her head on the bed railing when I threw her to the floor."

I couldn't believe I was listening to him say this!

In all seriousness, I said, "did you leave her there on the floor? We have to go back and help her Jeremy!"

When we made it back to his dorm room, thank God she was waking up. I stood in front of him and looked him dead square in his eyes and said "J, man. We need to get her to the hospital!"

He agitatedly responded saying, "what are we going to tell them happened to her? They won't believe us no matter what we say."

"J, relax man it's going to be okay. Let's go," I said.

We made it to the hospital. Looking at Jeremy, I said, "once we get in there, you need to try and clear your thoughts, so it won't reflect on your face what really happened. You may not want to mention the pregnancy, but you have too!"

Crystal was able to walk with the assistance of Jeremy holding her up. We got through the automated doors of the emergency entrance passing the police and headed straight to the nurses' desk. My heart was pounding, which meant Jeremy was in shambles. Looking over, surprisingly he was calmer than me. What he said next shocked me even more!

"Excuse me, nurse. My girlfriend needs to be seen; she had an accident in the storm. We were headed out to have dinner and, in our dash, running to the car, she tripped and fell down the stairs and hit her head. I'm so glad it was not worse!" Relief coursed through his face, was he faking it?

The nurse promptly responded, "can I have her name and yours?"

"Her name is Crystal Stevenson and my name is Jeremy Stone."

"Okay, thank you! There is some paperwork that needs to filled out, while I take her blood pressure and get her set to go back and see a doctor. Was there anything else we needed to know or should check?"

Jeremy glanced over at me in despair, and I knew what he was about to say so I gripped his shoulder and said, "she will be okay!"

"Yes, ma'am. She is pregnant, I'm sure how far along she is," Jeremy said.

"Okay, sir. We are going to get her back to see a doctor and get her checked out," the nurse said.

After the doctor examined her, we found out that Crystal couldn't remember what happened from temporary memory loss from hitting her head. Also, we were in total dismay to find out after all of that, Crystal was not pregnant! The doctor said it was what they call a phantom pregnancy. This is when there are clinical or subclinical signs and symptoms associated with pregnancy when the person is not actually pregnant. Needless to say, the relationship ended. That made Jeremy know even more on how he felt about having kids. Although, I still believe to this day that there is more of an underlining issue to why Jeremy is the way he is, which he has never mentioned to me. I know one thing; I will never forget that night!

8   Lisa Maxton

While standing in the mirror applying my make-up, I could tell I was still agitated at the fact that Sheila doesn't deserve Jeremy. As fine as he is. Then, he has the nerve to be concerned about her when she can't even open up and be honest with him! So again, I do not feel bad one bit that I am trying to push up on her man, because I have seen her do some dirt. I guess I can say she is my girl and all, but what goes around comes around.

As I was putting the finishing touches on my make-up and blotting my lipstick me, my phone started to buzz. It was Shelia!

"Hey, Sheila! what's up girl, what's going on?" I asked.

"I'm sorry I didn't call you back last night."

"Nah, you're cool. At least I know you are still alive," I said nonchalantly. "So, what happened when you met up with Kenny?"

"I told him to meet me in the parking garage across from the hotel, because I didn't want to take a chance of Jeremy seeing him. Anyway, I basically told him there was not going to be anymore us. Also, I told him that he was not going to ever see Micah again if he kept being abusive towards me. I don't want my son to pick up any of those traits. If it is verbally, mentally, or physically abusive, he does not need to see any of it! I also hope it does not come naturally to him as he gets older, because Kenny is his father," she said.

"So, what did he have to say to that?" I asked.

"He raised his hand to me like he was going to back slap me, but somebody pulled into the ramp where we were. He hurried up and jumped back in his car and pulled off. You know what freaked me out before he pulled off, he had this crazed look in his face and said that it was not going to be the last time I saw him," she said.

"Is it bad to say that I am almost wishing that something terrible happens to him? I just want him out of me and Micah's life. This really makes me regret ever getting involved with him. The only good thing that came out of this was having Micah!"

"So where is Micah?" I asked. I was hoping she was going to slip up and tell me where he was, because she never really talks about it. But the more information I have about Micah, the more I will be able to work against her.

"Come on, Lisa. You know I don't discuss Micah, at any means. I keep my baby very secure," she said.

"I'm sorry, girl. I know your sensitive about that part of your life."

"It's not that I'm sensitive. I'm just being smart and very cautious," she said.

"So, were you able to get some rest when you got home?" I asked.

"Yeah, Eric called me and took me to the Oasis Spa, which was so relaxing. He rubbed my feet. It was just what I needed. I didn't want to stay at my house, so we went to his place and stayed. He is really a good man. That is the main reason why I have to nip this Kenny situation in the butt."

"Why didn't you want to stay at your house? Were you scared of Kenny showing up at your house again?" I asked.

"No not really, but with him you never know."

Why was she acting like she wasn't worried that Kenny would show up again, when I know she was? She didn't have to save face for me!

"Well, I'm glad to hear you're okay! I guess I will see you later today."

"All right girl, I will talk to you later. Bye," she said.

"Oh, Sheila! Wait, hold on. Before you go, I have been hearing things around the office that Michelle is going to have a Birthday party this weekend. Will you be going to her event?" I asked.

"You know Eric and I will be there to get our groove on!" Shelia said.

"Anyway, let's catch up at lunch or either meet later today?" I asked.

Now that I know that Sheila and Eric are going to be there, I'm going to have to set my plan in motion and pull out that "come and get it" dress I have that accentuates all of my curves. I saw how Eric was looking at me today. He is not happy and he knows he wants to taste this. I can just imagine his hands on my body working me down! I had a missed call on my cell, and whoever it was left a message around the time I was talking to Sheila. I did not recognize the number, so I was curious to find out who it was.

"You have one new voicemail, please enter your pass code. Hey Lisa! It's Eric. I need to talk to you, give me a call at 428-7509."

Well, well, well. I know exactly what I'm going to do to push this situation out in the open. I'm not even going to call him back. I will get with him at the party! I punched in a different number.

"Hey, Kenny. It's Lisa," I said.

"What's up, girl?" He asked.

"Listen, you got any plans this weekend?" I asked.

"Why?" He said.

"Sheila told me what's been going on with you guys. You and I go way back!"

"Yeah, so are you going to tell me what's up and stop beatin' around the bush?" Kenny asked.

"I know you want Sheila back, right?"

"You know I can't live without that girl," he said.

"Okay. On Saturday, one of our colleagues is having a party. I need you to come down here, so Sheila won't be able to go because when you show up, she always blows off the guy she is with. That way I can get at him, because he has already been hinting at me about why she is always blowing him off. I think he is really getting tired of it, and I think he is going to let her go. I'm going to help him push his decision on along quicker than he expects," I said slyly.

"Damn, girl. That's scandalous. I thought she was your girl. Does she talk about my son?" He asked.

"She is cool, but I have to look out for myself. No, she doesn't talk about Micah. she keeps his where-a-bouts under lock and key! Besides I owe you one anyways from when you and your crew took care of that guy who was beating me up when I was with him," I said.

"Awe, girl. That was nothing! Just call me later tonight when you find out the rest of the details," Kenny said.

"Okay, Kenny. I will call you later, bye!" I said.

I will never understand why girls like Shelia get good men. Eric literally is pinning after her and trying to understand why she can't fully love him like he loves her. Of course I get the men that want to dominate me and try to beat my ass when they feel like it or see fit!

I know I deserve more. It all boils down to when I use to witness my mother deal with all different abusive and possessive men as a young girl. I always attract the same men as she did. At least I refuse to have a life like that and think it is okay! It was like this for a while, not knowing who she was going to be inviting to dinner or going out with! She was constantly introducing me to different man. Telling me to be nice and to smile saying this is mommy's new friend! This all stopped when Derek came along. When they first met he was really sweet. He would come over early mornings in the winter and wipe off my mom's car, start it up, shovel the driveway, and have breakfast brought to her before she went to work. He started to spend the night, leaving his clothes at the house, and parked his car in the driveway. She was so happy for a long time until the fairy dust seemed to wear off in this relationship.

I was 16 when the sunny days for my mom turned into stormy clouds with Derek. It all started when he lost his job, and he stayed at the house claiming he was looking for work. It was like my mother was under his spell. When she would come home from work, he was either laid up on the couch with his drink or sprawled across her bed. I watched her cater to him. She would wash his clothes and make him dinner to just keep him around. At least that is what I thought it was, until I walked up on my mother standing at the kitchen sink with tears streaming down her bruised face.

At that point, I knew she was afraid to say anything about it, let alone put him out. This made me angry and afraid for her more. I wanted to harm him in his sleep! I would always ask her how long it has been going on and she would change the subject. It always bothered me because she could have bruises I couldn't see. Her body language was expressing to me to be quiet when I asked about the bruise and not make a scene knowing he was in the next room. All I could do was hug her and whisper in her ear and tell her that we have to get out of here. My arms embraced her around her back, I felt her flinch in pain.

She held me tight in return and said, "I will not let

him harm you. I will get us out of here!"

Some memories as a kid or a teenager, you are able to forget. Then, there are those that stay embedded in your brain. Within the next week, it was like he knew my mother was going to try and leave him, because he became even more sadistic than usual. He started to monitor her every moment of the day. He would call at her job and sometimes pop up there just to make sure she was there. My mother began to get used to his behavioral traits where she was able to avoid his dark thoughts towards her that lead to the physical abuse.

One night my mother not only freed herself, but she saved me as well. I saw how exhausted she was when I came through the door, she sat at the kitchen table slumped over with her head down. I cautiously tapped her on the shoulder, afraid of what I was going to see when she lifted her head to look at me. I put on a brave face. When she looked up, I could tell she had been crying, her mascara was running. Her lip was swollen and busted. Her right cheek was swollen with a cut under her right eye! I knew this was all from Derek. The cuts on her face were from the rings he wore on his right hand. I was so pissed; all I saw was red.

I turned to grab the biggest knife off the counter when my mother tightly grabbed my wrist to stop me. Her arm was shaking. That is when I saw the magazine from his gun in her other hand! I didn't know what to think, I was praying that I didn't see his body in a pool of blood when I walked into her room!

I hesitantly tippy-toed down the dark hallway towards her room. When I approached the door, it was slightly cracked. I took my right hand and slowly pushed the door open, as it made this creaking sound. I started to see his body laid across the bed. The lamps had been flipped over off the nightstand, clothes were all over the floor, and the only light that lit up the room was the streetlight breaking through the shades. I saw his feet dangling off the bed As I walked further into the room looking upon his unconscious body, I saw he had been shot in the shoulder. At the other side of the bed where his head and arms were on the floor, I saw a cast iron skillet on the floor. I knew then she hadn't killed him but knocked him unconscious. My mom called the police after she knocked him out. She pulled me out of the room and sat me down at the kitchen table. What she said still haunts me to this day.

She said, "honey, I had to. He was going to kill me then you when you got home!" As soon as she said that, the police were knocking on the door.

When the police arrived, I sat there quietly as my mother recalled to the police what happened. At that moment, I realized how strong my mother was to endure his abuse and sacrifice saving me. She knew more about his background than I thought! She had waited patiently over the past few weeks for this moment to arrive. She knew when she got home that he would already have been drinking Bacardi 151. She mentioned that she had headed right to the kitchen to start preparing dinner, when he emerged from the back of the house in a drunken stupor. When he approached her, he was breathing down her neck with assumptions that she was late getting home, because she had been with another man.

Before any response could be made, his hand was gripping her hair dragging her to the floor down the hallway to the room. She said she was fighting to break loose from his grip until she caught her footing and was able to stand up. She knew he kept his gun in the nightstand on his side of the bed, so she ran to get it when he grabbed the tip of her foot making her fall into the nightstand. She was able to pull the drawer open and grab the weapon and upon turning around he was right there saying I'm going to kill you and your daughter! She had no choice, but to shoot him. She didn't want to kill him. She wanted to stop him, which is why she shot him in the shoulder. When she did it, it caused his body to turn towards the bed landing face down, she noticed he was still moving so she ran back into the kitchen and grabbed a cast iron skillet. She came back into the room and hit him once on the head, knocking him out!

After my mom told what happened, the police handcuffed her placing her in the back of the squad car to further investigate. The paramedics were able to resuscitate Derek. He was handcuffed to gurney when he became conscious. Then, he was taken to the hospital. After everything settled down, the police found out that Derek had a warrant for his arrest in another county for domestic violence. That women was not as lucky. He had beat her so bad that she survived three days in the hospital before passing away. Finding Derek allowed the police to convict him, my mother was released. His charges were upgraded to Second Degree murder and Second-Degree Battery. These are memories I will never forget!

9 Jeremy Stone

Fridays are usually slow for me. There's not too much work to be done, besides go over the blueprints throughout the week. Over the years, I tended to block out my crazy college past hoping that part of me would not resurface; but at times, I feel it stirring up in me. My mind has been on Michelle, so I decided to give her a call. No sooner than I was about to pick up the phone, Eric called. I knew what he wanted before I even picked up the phone.

"Hey Eric, what's going on man?" I asked.

"I don't mean to bother you again about this, J. But, did you think about what I asked you do for me the other day?" Eric asked.

I really didn't feel like getting mixed up his shit. But I had to think about what if it was me in this situation, I would want to know the truth too!

"Yeah man, I thought about it. I will help you out. Give me the information I need to know. We can probably set up something this weekend at Michelle's get together," I said.

"All right, man. I owe you one big time," he said.

"Yeah, you do. Just give me a call later today."

"Okay! I absolutely will. I'll holla at you later," Eric

said.

Eric better be right about this girl, because he has always been a little too forgiving when it comes to Sheila. I went ahead and called Michelle after I got off the phone with Jeremy.

"Hey, Ms. Sullivan. How are you feeling today?" I smiled.

"Good, I'm surprised to talk to you today!" She exclaimed.

"Why you say that?" I asked.

"I don't know. We had such a good time last night. I thought you would have been playing hard to get afterwards, like most men do," she laughed, adding, "I was not expecting to hear from so soon that's all, but I was going to give you a call today to ask if you wanted to hang out with me further after my gathering this weekend?"

"My boy needs me to take care of something for him. I actually think they will be at your party? You know Sheila Petty, right?" I asked.

"Yes, I do know her!" Michelle said.

"It's such a small world," I said.

"It's going to be at the Honeysuckle U again with

82

some of my close friends and co-workers. As I mentioned, it would make my whole birthday complete if you were able to hang out with me afterwards," she said with a nervous laugh.

"I think I could arrange that," I said. With your fine chocolate ass that is!

"What time do you want me there and would you like me to bring anything? Do you have any special request Miss. Sullivan?" I asked.

"No, you coming will be a special request in itself! Also, everything probably won't start to kick off until after 8:00 pm. And, don't forget to bring your dance moves with you because this birthday girl will want a special dance from you," she said.

"I can definitely do that! I look forward to it," I smiled.

"All right, Mr. Stone. I will see you tomorrow night. You have a good rest of the day," she said.

I have to make sure I'm looking GQ for her, because I'm sure she is going to be sexy as hell when I see her. Let me call Eric back to see if he could meet me there so I can see what Sheila and get the scoop on her.

"Hello. Hey Eric, man. Listen up, I'm going to be at the Honeysuckle U on Saturday after 8:00 pm for

Michelle's party. Can you show up there with Sheila so we can set something up?" I asked.

"Yeah, man. That would work!" He said.

"Since there are going to be a lot of people there, call me to let me know exactly when you guys will be there so I'll look for you. Then, you can find me later in the night and I will get everything I need from you," I said.

"Yeah, man that sounds like a solid plan."

"A'ight, man. I will see you there, bye," I said.

If all goes well with Michelle the night of her party, I'm going to take her to the Camelot Hotel. I know she has her own place and I have mine, but this is a high-class hotel. I hope she doesn't get the wrong idea for me just meeting her. She must be amazing if I'm thinking about taking her there it's a five-star hotel. Of course, I did some research about the hotel. They have Superior Egyptian Cotton 1500 thread count sheets on the beds in the suites, flat screen TV's on the walls, and a Jacuzzi tub with Egyptian cotton bath towels.

I didn't plan on telling Kyle because I'm not trying to hear him talk crap about it. I know he is going to say that it's too soon to be spending money like that on her, but I will tell him after the fact, that's if I tell him at all. Some of the girls I was with before weren't worth half the things I did for them. As a matter of fact, he introduced me to them, but he is still my boy though. I know he didn't mean any harm. My phone started to buzz, speak of the devil. Kyle is calling me now.

"Hey. What's up, Kyle?"

"Damn, I am glad it is Friday, because I am not getting any work done," he said. "Are you ready to get your party on at Michelle's gathering this weekend?"

"Yeah, man. But get this, Eric is going to be there with Sheila, and I told him it would be good time to scope her out. I could probably use you as a diversion because there's going to be a lot of people there. He needs to tell me about her so I can get started with this side investigation. I just hope it is not a waste of time, you know what I mean?" I asked.

"Well, you'll find out eventually. You always do. But, keep me posted."

"I will, because I have a weird feeling about all of this. Listen, I'm going try to get some work done before the rest of the day gets away from me," I said.

"Yeah, I should too. Catch you later!" Kyle said.

As I tried to get some more work done before the weekend, I could not help but think about everything that could possibly go wrong over the weekend. The last thing

I would want to do is ruin Michelle's party. What if this Sheila does have someone on the side and he shows up at this party stalking her! I have seen it happen before, and I have learned not to put anything past anyone. You never know what someone is capable of. Including myself, I will never forget what I did to Crystal and how I never saw her again after that incident. I know to this day, the way I treated her has to do with my secret. A dark, terrible secret. I have never told to anyone, and I don't think I ever will. I never thought my father walking out on my mother and me. As a kid, I would never have guessed the effect it would have on my mother and me. I know I have had a dark cloud over me since...

I stood at my office window looking out over the city and I thought back to that faithful day my life changed, and the dark cloud descended over me. I was 12 years old when the constant fighting started between my parents. Of course, as a child I didn't understand why. All I knew at the time was that we lived in the house, which seemed to be a castle. There was so many rooms. We had a pool in the back and I had my own playroom, which kept me occupied. Today, I realize that my parents had a playroom to keep me out of their hair.

My dad had a room that was decorated with a lot of sports memorabilia, he would go there to relax, watch football, or play pool. I guess I never really paid attention to the fact that when my dad was home, he spent all his time in that room and my mother was in hers, which was big enough for a small apartment with a walk-in closet. This is where I would often see her get all dressed up preparing for a special evening, but she never ended up going anywhere. She never knew I saw her wiping her tears, peeking through the crack in the door. I saw the pain in her face.

Back then, I thought my father was going on one of his many business trips, to which I ended up finding out he was not to return. I stood at the end of the hall watching my mother pleading and arguing with my father grabbing him by the arm, trying to keep him from leaving. As a child, the picture being portrayed in front of you is something you never really understand what you're looking at until you're older and you replay it in your mind.

As time went on, things began to dwindle and disappear at home. My playroom was not my playroom anymore my toys were gone. I went down the hall thinking I would see my father in his lounge chair watching football, but when I pushed the door open the emptiness of the room made the creaking sound even louder. I knew then he wasn't coming back, and this created an emptiness in me. I began to be closed off from people. Which, I witnessed firsthand the drastic change of my mother when my father left.

The other side of town is where we ended up, in a one-bedroom apartment over a thrift store. When we moved into the apartment, it looked so rundown the walls were painted a dingy tan color, the curtain rods were bent, the curtains were very thin, and the rug was a chocolate dark brown. I had to make the living room my bedroom by sleeping on the couch. The actual bedroom was very small. My mom could only fit a twin sized bed in there with a small TV on a stand. She did the best she could with redecorating to make the apartment look more like a home. Being in the inner city was completely different from what I was used to, it had begun to eat my mother alive. The area we lived in was considered to be a well-known drug distribution. I would often see used drug needles and crushed crack valves on the ground on my way to school.

Days turned into weeks, weeks into months, and then months into years. I started to notice items were disappearing from the apartment by the time I was getting ready to turn 15. I thought my mother was trying to make ends meet. It was much darker than that, because she started to disappear just as much. When I did see her, she was wearing the same clothes she had on four days ago. The needles from the streets had creeped into our house and taken over my mother's life.

I watched her change in front of my eyes. Her healthy figure began to frail. There was never any food in the house anymore. I often found myself lurking around the corner store to boost me something to eat. I think either it was luck or a guardian angel keeping me from getting caught. My mother didn't know over the last year I had been in touch with my grandparents, my mother's parents whom she had not spoken too in years. They tried to help her get clean multiple times, but she refused. The drugs had such a hold on her! She tried to drag me further down with her. It was like she wanted to dim the light I had left in me for good.

One day, I went with her. She said she wanted to go to the corner store and get some snacks, but she had to make a stop first. Since it was my mother, I did not question her. I should have known what we were doing because when we walked down this grimy back alley, I started to get nervous. On a gloomy day like that, it would have made any 15-year-old boy nervous! I was even more hesitate when I saw the abandoned building we were about to enter. This building had five floors with most of the windows busted out, some were boarded up, just like the back door on this place.

The board was slightly detached enough for people to enter. It was like a forbidden territory only the tainted were allowed. As she pushed her hair back with her hand and wiped her running nose, she looked at me and said this will only take a minute. I watched her starting to fidget, scratching the bend of her arm. The smell that smacked you in the face once inside was unforgettable. You saw unrecognizable people with sores on their faces and bodies. They were laid on top of trash and dirty rat-infested mattresses. The smell of musk, body fluids, and fire ironically filled this place, even with broken windows. On the third floor, we walked to the end of the hall and it was the last room on the left. I was afraid of what was behind that door. She stood in front of the door and called out the name Ernesto. Who I later found out was known to any crackhead as Ernesto Chavez, the next in line to take the reins.

He wasn't in the room by himself, he had two of his goons with him. Both men were Hispanic and stood around 6 ft tall with a muscular build and were dressed in all black! Ernesto Chavez was a Hispanic man who stood about 5'11", dressed in all black with his hair slicked back, and a goatee.

When he saw who was on the other side of the door, he smirked and said in the smuggest voice I ever heard, "Irene, you dirty bitch. I knew you would be back."

He didn't care that I was standing there. I would soon find out that she brought me there for collateral damage! He grabbed her by the face and pushed her to floor saying, "I know you don't have no money, so why are you here?"

I stood there in shock as I watched my mother plead at this man's feet, grabbing his pant leg begging for a fix. She turned and looked at me with desperation, and said, "baby, come over here so you can help momma get her medicine!"

Crawling on her knees to me, scratching and fidgeting she said to me, "baby, all you have to do is make him happy."

As I looked down at her my eyes filled with tears from anger, my heart for my mother was gone. She continued to beg, when I looked up and saw one of his goons walking towards me, unzipping his pants saying in a raspy voice with a strong accent, "come here, kid. Get over in the corner and make me feel good."

I broke away from my mother and ran for dear life. As I ran, I could hear her screaming in pain. I honestly don't know what happened to my mother after that day. I ended up living with my grandparents, sparing them the details about their daughter at her lowest point in life. As I got older, sometimes I thought I would see her on the street and maybe it was just wishful thinking. Memories can haunt your mind and scorch your life!

"Kim, hey girl! Are you busy, I need to talk to you?" I said.

"No, but I didn't expect to hear from you until later in the evening. You okay? You must have had a very tasteful evening with Jeremy huh!" She exclaimed.

"You freak. Yes, I'm okay. Girl, you just don't know that man. WOOOOOOO, it's like he had the blueprint to my body," I said laughing.

"Damn girl, it has been a long time! Let me know what went down. Spill it!" Kim said.

"First off, I invited him to my gathering and he said he will be there," I smiled into the phone.

"You called him?" She asked.

"Not today. He called me this morning to see how I was doing. I didn't expect to hear from him so soon, especially not the day after the date we had."

"What do you mean?" Kim asked.

"It was so romantic the way he held me. It was sincere, and we had a long conversation. When the date was over, he walked me to my car making sure I was safe before he went to his. I guess I'm not use to such a gentleman, and I know guys usually don't call until at least two days later," I said.

"Well, he might be the one if he is already acting different from them deadbeats you used to date. You better hold on to him!" She exclaimed.

"I definitely plan on it! So, you know what that means?" I asked.

"What?" She said.

"We are going to have to find me a very sexy dress tonight for tomorrow. I want it to say come and get me!" I laughed.

"Okay, you freak! Girl, you know I'm not going to let you down."

"Anyway, I know you have more juicy details of the story to tell me about your night," I said.

"I do, but you first," she laughed.

"All right, all right. He got to the hotel around 6:00 pm. We talked about things we liked, favorite colors, and middle names."

"So, what is his middle name?" Kim asked.

"Xavier. That is kind of catchy Jeremy Xavier Stone. Yeah it goes right along with all his rock-hard sexiness," I said.

"OOOOOOOOH, look at you! Okay, tell me more."

"Well, I found out he can cook and we were joking around about having a cook off, so you and Kyle will most likely will be the judges, all right?" I said.

"Okay, that's cool," she said.

"When we met up, we were out on the lounge area of the Volt bar. As I mentioned earlier, girl it was so romantic. So, he took it up on himself to go sit on the chase lounge that was covered in this private sheer tent. He told me to come over towards him. I didn't object to that at all, so I sat down and laid back on his chest as he wrapped his arms around me. As I sat in between his legs, butterflies rose in my stomach. And girl, he smelt so good. We talked some more. When the sun was setting it could not have happened at a better time, because I looked up at him and he leaned down and kissed me. It took my breath away girl!"

"I bet it did!" She said.

"The kiss we shared was magnetic and his hands started to caress my body. We had to remember where we were, it was like we were getting lost in each other.

Kim said, "if it got that steamy in public, what is going to happen when you're behind closed doors?"

"Girl, my thoughts have already gone there, thinking about where I'm going to put my tongue on his muscular body," I said, adding, "anyway after we kissed, the bar ended up turning on some old school slow jams. I went back to lay on his chest. Girl, he pulled me on top of him and all I have to say is the man sure does know how to use his hands. Nothing happened though we both decided to slow it down."

"Yeah right, girl! You know you got some!" She said.

"No, I want to take it slow with him. I like him a lot. He walked me to my car and said goodnight. Okay, now you spill it since you grilled me for all my juicy details."

"As you know, I sold the house. I made him shrimp fettuccini with chocolate covered strawberries. The music was playing, girl. I had the songs set for each part of the evening."

"What were you playing?" I asked.

"I had my girl Alicia Keys, Maxwell, and some jazz. He was telling me how he has fallen in love me all over again, so after dinner I told him to meet me in the Jacuzzi tub. You can basically tell what happened next."

"Girl, you better be careful I might be somebody's

auntie," I said.

"Oh girl, you know I'm always careful. Besides you have a man in your life now, I can see a baby in your future," she said.

"Okay, okay! I will stop teasing you! You know I'm there for you anyway no matter what. I'll call you later, so we can go shopping and out to dinner," I said.

"Okay, girl. Talk to you later," she said.

It was funny she mentioned me having a baby in the future, because I wanted to tell her about the weird dreams I had been having. The ones that I hear the laughter of a child and the voices. It will be better if I tell her in person that way, I can have her undivided attention. I called the restaurant for tomorrow to make sure that everything was ready.

"Honeysuckle U, this Kara speaking how may I help you?" The girl on the phone said.

"Yes, my name is Michelle Sullivan. I reserved your V.I.P party room. I was calling to see if everything I ordered arrived accordingly."

"Can you hold one moment please?"

"Yes."

A couple seconds later, she said, "Miss. Sullivan?"

"Yes, I'm still here," I said.

"Okay, we have an order for cream colored tablecloths, tea light lamps, the booths and chairs have already been cleaned and setup. Also, we have a case of Red Wine Merlot, a case of Peach Arbor Mist, and the shrimp and lobster will arrive fresh in the morning for your shrimp cocktail and crab cakes. The wings are already here and the salads would be made fresh when ordered. Does that sound good Miss. Sullivan?"

"Yes, that sounds great! Kara, you have been very helpful. Have a good day!" I said.

"Thank you! You as well, bye." She said.

Appetizers and salads will be fine. If they're still hungry after that, they are more than welcome to go to the restaurant that I like to call their refrigerator at home. Okay, that is all set now all I have to do is hope no one acts up at my party. Oh and I have to make sure my homeboy, Michael got all those invitations out for me. I dialed Michael's number.

"Hey Michelle, wassup girl?" Michael asked.

"Nothing much, I just wanted to check with you and make sure you were able to get all of the invitations out for me."

"I sure did. Everyone who got one said they would be there," he said.

"Okay, make sure you bring your girl!" I said.

"You know it, homie. If she is with me, you know it's going to be right."

"That's how you do it," I said laughing. "Thank You Michael!"

"No problem! Anything for you, Michelle, on your birthday. See you tomorrow!"

The weekend was finally here, and I was about to meet up with my girl at Nordstrom, and then get a bite to eat.

"Hey, girl. I'm standing at the entrance of Nordstrom, are you close to the mall?" I asked.

"Yes, I am parking my car. I'll be there shortly."

"Okay, see you in a bit!" I said as I ended the call. I waited for a couple minutes and then I saw Kim making her way towards me.

"Alright, I am here. Let's find you a sexy dress, what did you have in mind? Do you want to wear something long or short? Do you want it to be form fitting? Also, what color?" Kim asked.

"I know I want it to be form fitting, classy, and sexy. Above the knees in length, but not too short. Just enough to show off my diva legs! As for the color, let's see what pops out at me," I said.

"I know what would look really good on you. Let's go look at the bandage dresses."

"Kim, I am glad you came. I have been wanting to tell you something. Now, don't look at me weird when I say this!" I said.

"Why would I do that? What's wrong, Michelle?" She asked.

"Let's sit-down over here. I don't know what this means, but lately I have been waking up to voices and sounds," I said. With a look of confusion and concern on her face, she sat back and prepared to listen.

"It started happening a couple of weeks ago after I met Jeremy! I woke up to an eerie whisper in my ear, saying 'I'm cold, it's so dark in here!' It was not a voice of impious intent, but a voice of a small child. Even though it was the voice of a child, I was still freaked out by what it said and what does it even mean? I also heard laughter of a child one day when I was waking up from a nap. At first, I thought it was the TV because I fell asleep watching it, but it wasn't," I said.

"You said laughter?" She asked.

"Yes, you know the giggle a child gets when you're playing that little game 'here I come, I'm going to get you'?"

"Yes, I know what you're talking about," she said, the concern still all over her face.

"The laughter was like happiness running away and the sound fading," I shuddered.

She asked, "do you know who lived in your apartment before you? Do you know if they had kids or if something happened to one of them that used to live there?" She asked.

"I haven't done any research like that. That is a good idea, especially if this continues to happen." I guess I spoke too soon when I told her, "It's not like items are being misplaced in my apartment."

Little did I know, it was already starting to happen, and I didn't realize it. Still with a look of concern, Kim responded, "I usually don't believe in this kind of thing, but maybe this could also be a subconscious thought manifesting itself or a sprit wanting your help! A spirit?"

Okay now, I'm more freaked out then before Kim! I couldn't think of any other reason why this would be happening to me. It was the beginning of something way deeper tugging at my soul...

11 Sheila Petty

After spending the night with Eric, I felt like I was ready to tell him what's been going on in my life for the last two years we have been together. He deserves the truth. This was eating away at me. I am also afraid he won't love me the way he has grown to love me. Damn! I have put him through too much already and he has forgiven me; but this I'm not so sure about, he always talks about how he wants to start a family. Hearing this might just push him over the edge, I was thinking I can take him away for a nice evening tomorrow night after Michelle's party.

Then and only then, I will let him know. I want him to know how much I really appreciate him, and how he has changed my life for the better. Based on what I have been going through with Kenny, this has really made me open my eyes on the value of life and who I have that's willing to take a chance on me. I admit to myself I had to do some soul searching to do.

All I need to do now is make it through the rest of my day without any unneeded drama. All the meeting times were pushed back and ran a little longer today for some odd reason, since it was a Friday. I ran into Lisa again after the first couple of meetings we had in the morning, by this time it was a little after 2:00 pm already.

"Hey girl, are those meetings hectic today or what?"

Lisa asked.

"Hey, girl! Yes, they are hectic," I said.

"At least we are coming to the midpoint of all these group projects," she shrugged. "I know you are happy about that!"

I laughed, saying, "girl, yes I am."

"What's up, Shelia? Do you have any plans after work?"

"No, why?" I asked.

"Let's go shopping for the party tomorrow. We could get our hair done, a manicure, and pedicure, you know a whole spa day!"

I don't know why my intuition was telling me she was up to something, but maybe I am just being paranoid. I ignored my gut and I said I would go along.

"Okay, girl. That sounds like a good plan. I could use some fun and we haven't hung out in a while anyway. All right, Lisa. I'll meet you in the parking structure around 6:00 pm," I said.

"Sheila, I might be a little late so don't leave without me girl!"

"I won't! You ready to go back in for the rest of

the meetings? I heard we are probably going to have a late lunch," I said.

"Yes, I'm ready. Wait, let me run to the washroom first. I will be back!" Lisa said.

After a couple minutes of waiting, my patience was wavering. What could she be doing in there? Another minute went by, then she finally walked back into my office.

"I thought I was going to have to come in after you. What took you so long, you okay?" I asked.

"No! I'm fine. My stomach was feeling a little funny that's all, but I'm okay. Did I miss anything?" Lisa said.

"No, they just brought in lunch. I think they have some Sprite or 7up over there."

"That will work, I'm going to get me one of those. Hopefully, it will settle my stomach," she said.

The rest of the meetings kind of flew by, I was relieved about that because of the crazy week I had. I am going to enjoy the spa. No men, just me and my girl hanging out. Maybe Lisa is pregnant? I hope she isn't pregnant. If she isn't, I'm going to find out why she's been acting so strangely.

"Hey Lisa, I'm going to my office to put up some paperwork and I will meet you down in the parking garage. Are you feeling better?" I asked.

"Yeah, my stomach has calmed down quite a bit. How long are you going to be?"

"Not long, I have to finish up this list for the upcoming project. Five minutes at the most. Lisa do you know where I parked?" I asked.

"Yeah, on the third floor down by the west end elevators, right?"

"Yeah, see you in a couple of minutes," I said.

I got down to the parking structure and noticed that there was a light out three cars down from mine. I really didn't think too much about it, but something was telling me I should have reported it. I ignored my instinct and headed towards my car and got in. I was about to place my Jill Scott cd into my cd player when I looked up and there was a man sitting in my back seat with a half face ski mask on. He had on a black hooded sweater and some leather gloves on. He didn't say anything, he just sat there and stared at me!

My heart was pounding. I didn't know if I should scream or try to get out the car and run. But, he could have a weapon on him or not. All I could think about was being smart, because I have a little boy who needs me.

"Wha- wha-, what do you want? Is it money because you can take it all? If it is the car you can have this too, just please let me go! I have too much to live for!" I shuddered.

It was like every emotion I was feeling inside was boiling to my head that I could not let out, I couldn't even cry something inside of me kept me calm. He noticed me look at the clock in my car, because I was wondering where Lisa was and hoping her appearing would startle him.

When I began to turn around and question his motive again that's when he put both of his hands over the back of my driver seat gripping my neck saying, "do not turn around or I will hurt you." His voice was a little raspy. He then proceeded by saying, "I never thought the mother of my child would show weakness like this in a time of distress."

When I realized what the assailant had said, it clicked to me who it was, and it made me snap.

"KENNY? YOU PUNK ASS BASTARD! WHAT THE HELL IS YOUR PROBLEM? WHY CAN'T YOU LET ME LIVE MY LIFE!" I yelled.

"Because I own you, you didn't know that?" When he said that I lost it, all I could think about was surviving for Micah. I grabbed my stun gun on the side of the driving seat and went after him in the back seat. He noticed the stun gun in my hand and leaped out of the car before I could get a hold of him! I got out of the car behind him and did not want to make a big scene in the parking lot, as I watched him run down the ramp and disappear. I think Kenny got the picture that I was fed up with his bull crap.

This was starting to become a pattern with him meeting me at my car or showing up at my apartment, I had to put an end to this madness. One thing for sure is I am definitely going to take that tint off the back windows, this is ridiculous. I called him knowing he could not have gotten far, and probably was still lurking around.

"Kenny, what do you want me to do get a restraining order on you? Are you crazy?" I asked.

"No, but I do want to see my child. I will see my child by any means necessary! Sheila, you seem to forget that I have contacts everywhere. I can find my son if need be, but I'm giving you a chance to take me back so we can be a family again. My patience with you is really running thin," he said.

"Kenny, I don't want anybody to get hurt. Maybe we can work something out, but like I said before, you have proven to me time and time again that you are not a good father! I mean look at what you just did, you have been pulling some crazy stunts lately! That's not going to fly." I sighed, adding, "I don't want to talk about any of this now. I have prior engagements to attend to all weekend, so I would appreciate it if you were to leave me alone. I don't want to see you for a little while."

I expected him to blow up on the other end of the phone cursing and ranting when I said that, but surprisingly he kept his cool. He didn't respond and I noticed his car was parked down the ramp. No wonder I didn't see his car before, it was parked next to the concrete beam. By the time he was about to pull away in his car, the night security was passing through. I noticed that they got a look at him, and that wasn't the only thing I noticed. Kenny got out of his car and stood behind a post once the security passed to make sure I didn't stop them. I wasn't going to jeopardize anything. Karma will take care of him, I just got in the car and drove off. I didn't even bother to call Lisa. I went home and grabbed some things and headed to the Spa by myself. Lisa didn't even show up there and I wasn't surprised. I will see how she acts tomorrow when I see her at the party.

As I laid there enjoying my massage, I could not help but to still be angry at the fact that Kenny was sabotaging my life. The more I thought about it, the more I started to see red. I hate to say it, but I wanted something bad to happen to him. I was starting to hate and despise him. I didn't care if my son never knows who his father is.

I got a call from Eric which distracted me from my devious thoughts. As I prepared to answer the phone, it is now or never that I divulge the truth.

"Hello, hey babe!" I said.

"Hey babe, how was your day?" Eric asked.

"It was long for a Friday, we had meetings most of the day."

"Why do you sound like something is wrong, where are you?" He said.

"I am at the Spa. I was supposed to be meeting Lisa here, but she didn't show up. I decided to go ahead and get pampered." The line was silent. "Hello, hello! Eric are you still there? Why did you get quiet suddenly?" I asked.

"Yeah, babe. I'm still here, just paying attention to the road. There are some idiot drivers out here."

"You be careful out there, Eric. I'm actually glad you called because we need to talk. I have something important I want to tell you and you deserve the truth, so let's talk in person, okay?" I said.

"Okay, babe!"

He needs to know the truth; I just hope it won't ruin our relationship for good!

12 Michelle Sullivan

"Hey, Michelle! I am so sorry about last night, Kyle called, and he wanted round two. He knows how to make my body call his name!" She laughed.

"It's cool! Kim, you are crazy," I said laughing, "you are such a freak, that is all I have to say about that. What are you doing? Is your schedule clear today?"

"Nothing much. Of course, it is me and you girl. So what do you want to start with first?" Kim asked.

"I was thinking we could get our nails done and a pedicure, then we go get our hair done. I made us an appointment at Gee Gee's Pin it up Salon. We will be ready for that party!"

"That sounds like a plan. As long as we can stop and get some lunch in the plan, it would really be a good plan. I laughed and said, "we will be stopping to get something to eat, Kim. You are so silly!"

"So, anything going on at the Marriott, Michelle? Any drama?" Kim asked.

"Well, you know how rumors can spread around an office like wildfire. You know my assistant, Michael?"

"Yeah." She said.

"He told me that he was pulling through the parking structure a couple of days ago and saw Sheila with some guy who looked like he was being aggressive to her.

Michael drives through very fast. He said he scared him off, because the guy jumped in his car and drove off," I said.

"Will she be at your party tonight?" Kim asked.

"I don't know, maybe? I had Michael pass out some invitations to my party. He said everyone who received one said they would come, so we will see who shows up. I try to tell those girls that work at the hotel to be careful, especially with some of the men they mess around with. You never know what could happen. I've known Sheila for a little while now, but there is this girl named Lisa that she has been friends with for a while. I get an uneasy feeling about her. You know when you meet somebody and it's something you don't like about them and you just can't pinpoint it," I said.

"Yeah, girl. I know exactly what you mean. Well, I will tell you this you, point her out tonight and I will feel her out."

"Cool! Kim, I know I can count on you. Let's go out now, so where do you want to get something eat?" I asked.

"We can go right to Applebee's because the hair salon is not far from there. And besides, they have good lunch specials. Have you tried the steak covered with sautéed shrimp and melted cheese, it comes with a mashed potatoes and green onions and steamed broccoli? Damn, it's delicious," she said.

"I would have thought you were the chef, Kim," I said laughing.

"I'm just saying it is so good, you should try it. You know I was also thinking about what you told me last time we talked about the voices and the child's laughter, has it happened again?" Kim asked.

"I wasn't going to say anything, but it was even stranger this time. I will tell you while we eat lunch," I said. Twenty minutes later, we were sitting down at Applebee's.

"Hi, my name is Deshaun. I will be your waiter this afternoon, can I start you lovely ladies out with something to drink and an appetizer?" He asked.

"Yes, I will have Raspberry Iced Tea," I said.

"And, for you miss?"

"I will have the Pink Lemonade," Kim said.

"Okay, did you ladies need a moment to look over the menu for appetizers?"

"Yes please, thank you!" We got our drinks and ordered our food.

"So Michelle, are you happy with the dress we found yesterday?" Kim asked.

"Absolutely! The dress says live it, like it, love it and you know you want to taste it!" I said laughing.

"Damn girl!" Kim said laughing, "are you saying you are ready to love again or what?"

"I think so. Jeremy gives me the Jones in my bones and those hands. Wool!"

"Michelle, I don't know what I'm going to do with you, girl!" Kim said.

"I think you're rubbing off on me, Kim."

"What!" She said.

"Don't act like you don't know what I'm talking about. I said it once I will say again you are a freak!"

"Whatever! On a more serious note are you ready to tell me what happened?" Kim asked.

I took a deep breath, and said, "okay, I'm ready. It happened the same day I heard the laughter. I didn't focus on it until later. Before I completely woke up that day, I felt a tugging on the pillow I was sleeping on and that it was in a different position than before. I know you might think I moved it in my sleep, but you can tell it was pulled on. Also, there was a teddy bear that I had sitting on my accent chair that had been moved to the end of the couch. I know what you said before, but I feel like it something deeper connected to me my spirit. I don't feel it is a spirit of another child.," I said.

"Michelle, whatever this means. I am here when you need me. I know this can be scary for you and I could not imagine experiencing something like this! We should finish up our lunch, so we can go get our hair done."

It was getting close to our appointment time. I said, "yeah, you are right. Time has flown by, I love how Gee Gee's does my hair."

"So, how are you enjoying your meals ladies? Can I get you anything else?" The Waiter asked.

"Yes, it was delicious. We would also like the bill and some boxes, please and thank you," I said.

"Sure, I will be right back."

"Michelle, what are you going to get done to your hair?"

"I'm going to get a bone straight wrap," I said.

"Oh, that should be cute!"

"What about you?" I asked.

"I'm thinking a wet set," she smiled excitedly. We got our bills and boxes. "All right, girl. Let's roll out. We still have to find some shoes to go with that sexy dress you bought."

"The day is getting away from us, it's almost 2:00 pm. Kim, I know exactly where I want to go get my shoes!"

"Where?" She asked.

"Her name is Jaidore. Whenever I need a pair of banging shoes; I go to her and she hooks me up. She is only a little older than us, and the girl is fly. She has got it together. It's called Jaidore's Lady Love. It's right downtown on Grand River Avenue."

"That's cool! We can go there after we are finished getting are hair done."

We walked into the hair salon and Gee Gee came up, "hey ladies, how are you today?"

"Good, Gee Gee. How are you?" I asked.

"You know me, making you ladies more beautiful is my thing. I think April is ready for you, Michelle. Kim, Taylor will get you started."

That's why I like coming to Gee Gee's, you're in and out. I always give a generous tip to my stylists and set up my next appointment, I try to go every two weeks. Before I left, I invited them to my birthday party. I added, "So, everything most likely will jump off around 9:00 pm."

"All right, Michelle. We will see you there."

"Thanks again, Gee Gee! See you ladies tonight! Get ready to have a good time," I smiled broadly. "Okay, it is around 4:00 pm. We still have time to get over to Jaidore's and get some shoes."

"Michelle, tonight is going to be fine! No worries, there is not going to be any drama. What you need to worry about is that sexy man of yours showing up and giving you the night of your life!" Kim said.

"Whatever, Kim." I laughed.

"Don't whatever me, Michelle. You know I'm right. That is why you're laughing and smiling like that. We're here, so let's see what your girl has for us."

"Hey, Michelle. How have you been? Good, Jaidore. This is my best friend Kim. Kim, this is Jaidore." I said.

"Hi, nice to meet you! Looks like you have some very tasteful shoes here. When you called me to let me know you needed something for your party tonight, which by the way thank you for the invite. I pulled out quite a few pairs that the shop has gotten shipped here from Miami. I think you'll like it, I will be right back," she said.

"Okay. All right, Michelle. I know you already picked a dress for your party, but this black dress would look great on you!" Kim exclaimed.

It was long dress that had a V-neck plunge in the front that will show off cleavage very nicely. It's a pullover dress, so it ties behind the neck. As the dress goes down, it form fits around the waist and hips. On the left side of the dress, right in the hip area there is a keyhole with a silver chain connected that goes down the thigh. Right where the keyhole is there is a slit that goes right up to it.

"Now for this next dress…" she added.

"Wait, I don't think I even want to see the next dress. Let me try this one on and see how it looks," I said with excitement. I wonder when she started selling dresses?

"Okay, that's fine! Go ahead and do your thing!" Kim said.

"Kim, have you found anything?" I asked.

"Yeah, I think I'm going to try this yellow dress on," she said.

"OOOH! That color would look great on you!" I said, we both went into changing rooms.

"Let's come out at the same time, okay?" Kim said.

"Okay!" I yelled through the dressing room door, "Kim, I am so glad we have been hitting the gym, because I am doing it in this dress!"

"Let me see, Michelle. Yes, I think we have found your dress!" She exclaimed.

"Not only did we find my dress, that dress looks good on you too, Kim!" I said.

"I like it too. I'm going to get it."

"All right, Jaidore. You have done it again, girlfriend. We love these dresses, and these shoes go perfectly with them!" I said.

"It is my pleasure, anytime! I will see you guys tonight." Jaidore said.

"Okay, thanks again, Jaidore! I'll see you later." I said, adding to Kim, "do you want to go my house and get ready there so we can ride over to the Honeysuckle U?"

"Yeah, that's sounds good. I will call Kyle to let him know that I'll arrive with you, but I also need to stop at my house first to pick up some things and makeup," Kim said.

"Okay, that's works! We can head over there."

13 Kyle Walters

"What's up, J?" I asked. "You gone roll with me over to the Honeysuckle U tonight?"

"I can, but I might need you to take me to get my car later. Where is Kim?" Jeremy asked.

"She has been with Michelle all day. They are going to ride over there together," I said.

"Yeah, man. I guess that's cool. Give me an hour and half to get ready."

"I can do that, so how do you think the night is going to turn out?" I asked.

"I'm hoping well. I got some things planned for her that I am hoping she would like."

"What do you have planned?" I said.

"Well another boy of mine works over there at the Camelot Hotel, and he gave me the hook up on one of the suites at the hotel. I thought it would be a nice idea to finish off her night with an evening at a five-star hotel," he said.

"Sounds good, man! Let me know how it is, I wanted to take Kim there just haven't had a chance yet," I said.

"Yeah man, definitely. I will even get you the hook

up like I got, just let me know when you want to take her," he said.

"Okay, sounds good. I will be at your house in about 45 minutes, I will blow the horn when I'm outside."

"All right, I'm going to call Eric real quick and see if everything is still on with Sheila coming to the party tonight. I will tell you about it when you pick me up."

"A'ight, man. I'll see you soon," I said. I wondering what is going on with Eric and Shelia. Is Jeremy going to take the job to some digging on Shelia?

After I got ready and headed over to Jeremy's house, before I knew it we were headed to the party.

"Damn, man. Your looking good I guess somebody is trying to impress a certain young lady tonight," I laughed.

"You know me, Kyle. It's in my nature to look good I definitely take pride in my appearance." He said.

"I know, but Armani from head to toe." I laughed.

"Hey man what can I say, I'm GQ even on a bad day. Enough about me, you're looking all dapper yourself! Anyway, it's going down tonight." He looked at me in a serious expression.

"What's going down?" I asked in a worried tone.

"Eric is going to give me the down low on Sheila. Even after he told me never mind, because she told him she had something to tell him. He said when he talked to her yesterday, it sounded like she was worried and fearful about something. I just hope that this girl isn't involved in something deeper that she can't handle." He sighed.

"So, how are you going to get started?" I asked.

"Well, I'm going to probably have to pull the work meeting to find out some personal one-on-one information about her and take it from there. We both have seen how some of these situations can turn out."

"You need some help, let me know. I'm here," I said. "Well, we are here do you see Michelle's car?"

"No, it's only 8:30 pm. She will probably be a little late. You know woman have to make an entrance." We laughed together.

"Yeah, I know. Kim has to make an entrance when I pick her up to go out, and we could be just going to the movies. But, she looks good every time I see her. Her nails and hair are always done," I nodded in appreciation. "Kim may make an entrance, but she is always on point, which I love that about her."

"All right, man. Let's go in and order a drink while

we wait on our women," Jeremy said.

"Our women!" My eyebrows raised, "so, you are claiming, Michelle. You seem pretty confident about this relationship going somewhere, huh?"

"Yeah, man. I'm really feeling her," he smiled a broad grin.

"Just continue to let things flow and see how it goes. No need to rush!"

With a little animosity in his voice, Jeremy responded, "what makes you think I am rushing?"

"J, man. I didn't mean it like that, I just want you to make sure this is what you want?" I asked.

Although, in my mind, I was really thinking about how no one knows the truth about his past and how he never talks about his parents. He is my boy, but at times you can tell he has an infected personality.

I seem to recall more events than Jeremy cares to remember, which he seems to have blocked out especially after the incident with Crystal. That was not the last time I had to come to his aid. Whenever he gets close to a woman, things tend to happen. Of course, after Crystal there were many more women, but one in particular grabbed my attention. Her name was Pamela. She stood about 5'9", had a caramel complexion, and long sandy brown hair. She was very curvaceous with full lips and natural hazel-green eyes.

She had him open, but the problem was she was already involved with someone when she became acquainted with Jeremy and he didn't know! Eventually the truth came out, and this became a serious issue for him. It all started with just cordial conversation, because she would come into the store where he worked quite often. The next thing you know he was introducing me to Pamela, this "African American beauty", as he called her. It was all he talked about. They were spending a lot of time together whenever he was free. Apparently, she was balancing her time with Jeremey and her current boyfriend, Richard, until the two worlds collided.

Eventually Richard became suspicious when Pamela started to cancel when they had plans saying either she had to work late or go to a study session, he began to follow her. During this time, Jeremy had his own place off campus. It wasn't an apartment complex that had a secure entrance. Although after this incident, I wish it was. He lived on the second floor, right next to the stairs. It was very easy to access to anyone who may have wanted to know where he lived. Richard had followed Pamela all day up until the point where she ended up at Jeremy's apartment at 8:30 pm that evening. It was said that she stayed at his place for two hours before she decided to leave, and Jeremy walked her to her car before returning to his apartment. As mentioned before, Richard was sitting off in the distance watching all of this and he waited for Pamela to drive away. When Jeremy made it back inside his apartment that is when Richard got out of his car and headed towards Jeremy's front door to confront him.

As he approached the door, Pamela returned because she had forgotten her purse. When Jeremy opened the door, he was addressed by Richard with a gun to his chest, "so you are the punk ass that she has been sleeping with, huh?"

Jeremy stood there in disbelief at what was transpiring and said, "look man I don't know anything about you. If this about Pamela, she never told me that she was involved with anyone, bro! Just lower the gun so we can talk."

As soon as he said that, Pamela was coming back up the apartment stairs and caught Richard off guard by yelling out his name. "RICHARD, WHAT THE HELL ARE YOU DOING HERE?"

He then turned, pointing the gun at her, while Jeremy ran to call the police, "you didn't think I was going to find out, did you? You dirty tramp!"

"Richard, I thought you would have gotten the hint by now that I don't want to be with you anymore," she said firmly.

With the gun still pointed at her, "so you choose this bitch ass over me?"

As Jeremy came rushing back to help Pamela, that's when he heard the gunshot ring out in the stairway. Richard had shot Pamela hitting her in the shoulder knocking her down the stairs from the impact, as he watched her body tumble down the stairs. Richard followed her ready to finish her off! As he pointed the gun at her, he was approached by the voices of four police officers saying, "drop the gun and put your hands in the air!"

Jeremy was standing at the top of the stairs watching in horror as Pamela's body laid at the bottom of the stairs seeming to be lifeless. The police secured Richard in handcuffs. He looked at the desperation and fear in Pamela's eyes, and he surrendered. Jeremy was questioned by the police as well, while Pamela was placed in the back of the ambulance and Richard was hauled away. When I made it over to his complex, I could tell he was shaken up at the fact of seeing Pamela's body laying at the bottom of the stairs and not knowing the outcome. I sat there and watched Jeremy get interrogated by the police. After he was questioned by the police, he was cleared of the incident with no charges.

We later ended up finding out that Pamela survived the shooting, but had severe nerve damage to her left arm. Richard was charged with assault and attempted murder and received 7 years in jail for his first offense. I didn't think that was enough for almost killing someone our justice system can really be questionable at times. After everything calmed down, I looked at my friend and knew there was a gloom from his past that has tainted his soul and it had a hold on him. I just hope that one day he would reveal what that is before an event happens that won't turn out for the greater good.

14 Jeremy Stone- The Party

"Your girl got the V.I.P looking pretty lavish, man! Like, she is a superstar!" Kyle said.

"I told you she had style, didn't I? She knows how to put a room together!"

"Yeah, man. You weren't lying. Let's go get us a drink and see if anyone we know is here," he said.

"You know, Kyle, I could use a Grey Goose right about now. I just have a feeling that tonight is going to be a little crazy," I said.

"Why you say that?" He asked.

"You know how Eric and Sheila are supposed to be coming...." I shrugged.

"So, all you have to do is get some info about the girl and you act like you haven't done this before."

"I know what you mean, but this time I have a feeling something is going to go wrong." I said.

"Well just play everything cool, and I'll play back-up if something goes wrong," Kyle said, adding, "speaking of playing it cool, which I know you do pretty well, they are here."

The club was perfect for any type of investigation,

because we were able to look down on everyone who came into the club. I saw Eric make his way over to where they were.

"Jeremy?" Eric said.

"Eric, what's going on?" I asked.

"Nothing much, man. Just ready to have a good time with my lady." He smiled. Eric played it off as if he never mentioned the stuff about Sheila. "I want to introduce you guys to my lady. This is Sheila, Shelia this is Kyle and Jeremy. I went to college with these guys."

"Well, it's nice to meet you guys! Have you seen the birthday girl yet?" She asked.

"No, not yet. We just got here not too long ago."

Kyle nudged me and I knew what he was doing, so I started in on the questions. "So, how do you know Michelle?" I asked.

"I work with her at the Marriott Hotel. I'm in the Marketing department. I've known her for a couple years now," she said.

Eric had walked away to get her a drink. The crowd was starting to grow, so I had a little time to talk with her. Kyle was starting to converse with some of the other guest. While I talked to her, I saw Kyle continuously look over here. He seemed to be watching her body gestures, so I continued the conversation.

"So, you're involved with the inner-city youth project. That's being constructed at my office."

"Yeah," she said with some curiosity in her face.

"Oh, my bad, I never said how I know Michelle. We have been on a couple dates."

"Ooooooh! So, you're the reason she has been walking around with high spirits?" She asked.

"Really? Well, that is good to hear." I couldn't stop the grin from entering my face. "Listen, I'm going to need to discuss some slogan layouts for this project. I'm going to have get in touch with Eric so we can set something up, does that work?"

"Sure, that will be fine! Anything I can do for the kids is fine with me."

Just when she was about to say something her face expression changed, and I know Kyle noticed it too, it was like she became enraged when she looked up and saw this other young lady walk in. I also noticed when she walked up to the other girl. It all changed like she had something up her sleeve, and by this time Eric was coming back with her drink.

What took Kyle's and my breath away was our women walking through the door. Michelle looked breathtaking in that black dress. Every other thought disappeared. The night will end perfectly at the Camelot Hotel, I'm just hoping she'll says yes. I went down to meet her and make sure I let her know just how amazing she looks.

I whispered in her ear how she was teasing me with her beauty as I subtly slid my hand up and down her curvaceous hip. She felt like butter in my hand, as I walked with her caressing the small of her back. Kyle was right there with me swooning over Kim. I bet he is going to marry that girl. I have never seen my boy all over a woman like he was with Kim.

"So, Miss. Sullivan. I have never seen anyone so beautiful, until I saw you tonight. You look amazing. Are you ready to have the time of your life tonight?"

She leaned in close to me letting her soft lips slightly touch my ear, and said, "I'm hoping you are going to make this a very memorable night for me."

Looking down into her beautiful brown eyes I responded with assurance. "Oh, I will. I aim to please."

"Jeremy, this is my beautiful best friend Kim Shavers from college. Kim, this is Jeremy!" Michelle said.

"Oh, girl. Please you are the gorgeous one tonight. Well, hello! Nice to meet you, I have heard a lot about you Jeremy!" Kim said.

"Good things I hope," I laughed nervously.

"Oh, of course. All good things! Anyway, we are here to have some fun. Let's get this party started!" Kim said.

"You know how time flies when you're having fun."

Before we headed upstairs, we all danced. the DJ
was playing Keisha Coles. Jeremy pulled me close and
swayed. Right after that song, the DJ went back further
and played some Kenny Latimore. It seemed like there was
nobody else there, but us, he smelled so good. Sometimes
when I think things like this is destined to be, turns out to
be the opposite. I quickly shrugged that thought away or
tried to at least. I didn't want the song to end, even though
I knew it wasn't going to be the last time I danced with
him.

The night continued as I mingled with some of
my co-workers and thanked them for coming. I felt like I
was glowing. I was having such a great time. As the party
progressed, we all sat down to eat and I introduced Kim to
the ladies I work with. Everyone was enjoying themselves,
when I noticed Sheila and Lisa off over in the far corner
having what it looked to be a confrontational conversation.
I didn't want my party to go sour and I wasn't going to
tolerate it! Just when I was about to go over to disperse
whatever was brewing between them, Jeremy grabbed
me and spun me around towards him. I don't know if he
noticed them, which he probably did because he seems
to be very observant. He quickly averted my attention
elsewhere by asking me to spend the rest of the evening
with him at the Camelot Hotel. I looked at him with

disbelief, because the Camelot Hotel was the high-class hotel in comparison to Waldorf Astoria Hotel in New York.

Every other thought in my head erased. I was speechless. I finally snapped out of it when he smiled and said, "I told you I aim to please? Michelle, you deserve it."

"I accept your invitation. I will be your Guinevere tonight, but for now let's dance. I have only one objection. I have to go home after the party and grab some clothes," I said.

"No, you don't. It has already been taken care of. I don't want you to have to worry about anything this is your day!" Jeremy said.

Shelia Petty

"Sheila, I didn't expect to see you here!" Lisa said. You could hear animosity in her voice.

Out of curiosity, I asked her, "why would you say that, Lisa? Yesterday we were supposed to hang out, but I couldn't find you. Lisa, we said we were going to meet me in parking structure. I was waiting for you for 20 minutes and you never showed up. What happened to you?"

I didn't want to mention anything about Kenny to her, because she has been known to start some drama. Apparently, which she was trying to do now at the wrong place and time. When she answered me, you could tell she was trying hide something.

"Sheila, girl, I tried to call you. I kept getting a busy signal, so I left it alone. I figured you would call me whenever," Lisa said.

Lisa was being guileful. It made really want to whoop her ass right then and there. Later on that night, I noticed her body language towards Eric. I kept my composure at Michelle's party. It was her night and I didn't want to mess anything up for her. I will deal with Eric later. I thought Lisa and I were cool. Well, I guess that goes to show sometimes people outgrow each other. I ended up walking up to her. I couldn't take it anymore.

"I don't know what your problem is, but I'm not going to deal with this right now. I will tell you this though. If I find out you have any involvement with what's been going on in my life, because I know you can be trifling like that, you will have hell to pay!"

I walked away not giving her a chance to even respond, but I knew she was a vindictive person.

15 Michelle Sullivan- The Camelot Hotel

I noticed that there was still a strong tension in the air between Sheila and Lisa when my party was ending. I thanked everyone for coming and prepared to go over and speak to Sheila about what I saw to make sure everything was okay! As I walked towards her, she was walking away from Lisa, and you see the anguish on her face as I got closer. Of course, she tried to play it off as I hugged her and thanked her for coming.

I asked her, "Are you guys cool?" I gestured between her and where Lisa was standing.

"Yeah, girl. I'm good. Lisa is being Lisa. You know how she can be!" She shrugged.

"I understand. I know she can be a deceitful bitch at times, but don't let that ruin your night Sheila."

"I'm not. I am about to go find Eric and enjoy the rest of my evening with him."

"That sounds good, girl. I think I saw him over by the bar."

"Okay, thank you! Well, you be safe. I will talk to you later!"

As I watched her walk away, I felt Jeremy come up behind me wrapping his hands arounds my waist and he kissed me on my neck. Then, he spun me around by my hand and asked, "Are you ready to end your birthday the right way?"

My mind when back to Lisa and Shelia. I can find out what was really discussed between them on Monday when I get to work. I didn't really feel like listening to any drama on my special day anyway.

Kim yelled out, "Happy birthday, girl! I will call you tomorrow," she said with a broad grin as she left with Kyle!

"Okay, but not too early," I laughed. She better not call too early because as good as Jeremy was looking, I wanted to be wrapped up in him until we checked out.

When we arrived at the hotel, there was a pathway of lights that lit up the entrance. There were four sets of double doors that were a deep cherry wood with gold handles, which looked like they stood about 8 ft high. Each set of doors had a doorman that was dressed in uniform. All of them looked very professional with creases in their pants and not a button on their blazers was misplaced.

We received a warm greeting from the doorman as we approached, and I noticed Jeremy slip the doorman a tip. As Jeremy and I began to walk up to the front desk, you couldn't help but I noticed all the historical designs in the building. It was beautiful. The walls were very detailed in the structure. I was too busy paying attention to the design to even notice we were at the front desk.

"Hi, how may I help you this evening?" The clerk asked.

"Hello, my name is Jeremy Stone. I have a reservation for the night," he said confidently.

"Okay. Thank you for that information, Mr. Stone…" A few clicks later from the keyboard, "Oh, yes. I see you right here. You're set up for the suite with the city view. This view is very beautiful at night with all the city lights! A wonderful choice ! Is this a special occasion for you two?" She asked.

"Yes, it's this lovely young lady's birthday," Jeremy smiled.

"That is so sweet, and happy birthday to you! Oh, and I love your dress." The Clerk said.

"Thank you," I responded as a smile broke out across my face thinking this night could not get any better.

"Okay, here are your keys, Mr. Stone. There is room service that runs 24-7. If you have any questions, there is a stationary right next to the phone with all the numbers for service here at the Camelot Hotel. Enjoy your evening!"

This place was amazing. I never expected an

evening like this. This too good to be true! He was right when he told me earlier not to worry about anything because when we made it to our room, he had a duffel bag full of clothes for him and me laid on top of the bed.. The lights were out, but there tea light candles surrounding the tub in the bathroom. The bath was already full of water and bubbles. There were marble counter tops with double sinks with oval mirrors above each one. The sheets on the bed were Egyptian cotton on a huge Canopy bed. The colors were tangerine, gold, and crème. I was speechless.

Jeremy walked up behind me and nervously asked, "Are you okay?" I think he was getting worried since I haven't said anything in while because of how mesmerized I was by all the preparation he did for tonight.

"Yes." I smiled reassuringly. "I have always heard of this place, but I would have never imagined that it looked like this. How did you have time to do all of this, especially with the lovely gift bag, the candles, and the bath?"

"Well, I did tell you that I aim to please, didn't I?"

He continued to stand behind me when he said, "you're going to let your water get cold if you wait. This evening is all about you! Oh! Michelle, here. Don't forget your bag."

"Thank you," I smiled warmly.

I can't believe all this was happening. Jeremy and I only have known each other for a little while. My gut was turning into butterflies. I am going to enjoy this moment. I began to undress as I admired the calming effect of how gorgeous the bathroom was. There was a full moon and the glow shined in, reflecting off the tea lights. I slid down in the tub. The size of the tub was big enough for two people to fit in. The water was nice and hot. I had my hair pinned up so I could lay back and close my eyes. I felt like I had no worries in the world. I was so relaxed. My body began to float in the water.

As soon as it did, Jeremy knocked on the door saying, "you ok in there?"

I sat up with soap suds all over my body and said, "absolutely! You can come in, if you want?

He entered the bathroom with nothing but a towel on and said, "can I join you?"

How could I say no to all that goodness standing before me, especially with the light of the night illuminating off his body. The towel fell to the floor! There he stood in total confidence. I was right, he does work out. He was pure muscle as I stared him up and down. I noticed that he had a tattoo on the right side of his chest of an Aquarius sign. I tried to snap out of my gaze. When I did, he had a smile on his face that made me blush.

"So, Miss. Sullivan. May I join you?" He asked again.

"Yes! Yes, you can!" I said.

He walked slowly towards me and I slid back down into the tub spreading my legs for him to lay back in between. As I continued to watch him, his muscles weren't the only thing that was easy on the eyes. He had a very satisfying piece of equipment, which I hoped I would get to taste, touch, feel, and moan from every inch of it tonight. He stepped on down into the tub, and I told him to come down on my end so he could lie back on my chest. I told him how thankful I was and that everything was wonderful. I had never received such special treatment from a man.

"Michelle, I am glad to hear you like it. I know we have been only dating for little while. But when a guy meets a beautiful, intelligent woman and it's her birthday, he has to treat her! I don't know what your other birthdays have been like, but I wanted this one to be memorable for you."

I had my legs wrapped around his waist, while I began to rub the top of his head. We soaked in the tub in silence, letting our energy feed off of each other for a moment before he turned towards me and began to kiss me gently on my lips. Down to my neck he proceeded and before he continued to explore my body, he asked me if I was alright!

In the softest voice, I said, "yes, I am," as I laid my head back giving him permission to continue. I closed my eyes as he kissed and licked my breast seductively, sucking on my nipples. He pulled me up close to him as I mounted him, and I felt his pulsating thrust filling me up.

I moaned softly as I held him tighter. I whispered in his ear to go deeper! He did exactly that and I felt every bit of his muscle tone. At that moment, it felt so right being there with him. He moaned with a subtle growl as he continued to slowly stroke with his rhythmic movement. I didn't want to think of it being an infatuation, because I have been there before. This was different. I'm not going to think of anything negative. I'm just going to take it all in.

After a while in the bathtub, he stood me up so carefully and wrapped me in a towel. He carried me out to the bed. He laid me on my back and trickled warm body oil down the front of my body. His strong hands gently caressed every part of my body with oil. It was like he was massaging me at the same time. He had one hand on my breast lovingly rubbing the oil in and playing biting my nipples as his other hand worked its way down the rest of my body. After he was finished, he told me to raise my arms up and slid a satin chemise over me. I was in awe as I looked him in the eye, we climbed into bed and he just held me. Before I kissed him goodnight, I rubbed the side of his face and said, "thank you for this amazing night!"

"I am glad you enjoyed yourself. Anything for you, Michelle. Goodnight, sweetie."

16 Lisa Maxton

"Hello, hello. Kenny, what the hell happened to you tonight? Why are you just breathing into the phone and not saying anything like some psychopath?" I said.

"What!" Kenny said.

"You think someone is listening in? You got some nerve being paranoid all the shit you have done!"

"First thing, Lisa, shut the hell up. You always running your fuckin mouth! So, I think you need to change your tone of voice. I'm not one of those punk asses you used to talk too. I can see why you would get your ass beat."

"Alright, alright! Chill out, man. Damn, but everything was messed up tonight. Sheila and Eric showed up together. I thought you were supposed to keep her from coming, so I could get at Eric," I sighed.

"Don't worry about it, girl. Me and her are going to have another talk. This time this will be the last time I'm going to talk to her about seeing my son," Kenny grunted.

"Hold on. Now, Kenny I don't want you to hurt her or anything like that. I know how possessive you are," I said.

"Stop being so scared," he said laughing, "nothing

is going to happen to her, I'm just going to shake her up a little that's all."

"I only asked because she approached me tonight like she knew we were talking or something. It's like she is suspicious of what's been going on, but not saying anything. You know what I mean?" I asked.

"You know my Sheila is very observant. She is not dumb, that girl has got street sense. Listen, Lisa. I haven't even left town yet, I'm laying low around here. I will show my face again when the time is right, you know how I do!" He said.

"Yeah, you like lurking in the dark," I said.

"As for you, you better keep your cool. You will get what you want soon enough, just be patient," Kenny said.

"I hear you. You better be right. I will talk to you later!" I said.

I just might have to continue this on my own. I really do hope he keeps his word this time. I've known Kenny just as long as Sheila has, and he never really sounded so cool, calm, and collected about a situation. You never know with him though. I'm going to call Sheila and patch things over. You know what they say, keep your friends close, but keep your enemies closest.

Besides, she doesn't really know how acquainted

me and Kenny are. The phone began to ring when my line beeped, I didn't recognize the number. I answered it anyway.

"Hello," I said with an attitude. I had other things I needed to handle without someone calling to disturb me.

"Hey, girl. It's Eric, did I catch you at a bad time?" He asked.

When I heard his voice, my tone immediately changed. I have to keep fabricating my story to make Sheila actions look worse than he has already seen. Every time I see this man, he makes me hot under the collar, and my girl starts to purr.

"Hey Eric," I said sounding so sweetly, "how are you?"

"I'm good, and you?"

"Not too good!" I said.

"Why is that?"

"I know you probably saw Sheila and me arguing off in the corner last night at Michelle's party." I sighed dramatically into the phone.

"Yeah, that is what I was calling about to see what was up with that. Because you know she just blows things like that off, and says nothing is bothering her and I know it really is. I don't know why she feels like she has to be so tough all the time," he said.

"I know exactly what you mean, Eric. She has always been like that even when we were younger… What happened between us last night really hurt me because I thought we were closer than that."

I made it sound like I was really tore up inside, and the more I slathered on the deceit the more he was eating out of my hand. I said, "she just seems to be coming more distant lately. I say that because we were supposed to meet up the other day and hang out before the party and she was nowhere to be found nor was she answering her phone."

Although I knew the true reason why, Eric's silence indicated to me he was becoming more worried about the situation. In a true fashion, he tried to play it off, but I wasn't fooled one bit.

"Lisa, don't worry about it. Do you want me to find out what happened? Maybe I could talk to her?" He asked in a worried tone.

"No, I rather not. It just will make things worse between us. She will be wondering why I'm talking to her man about our issues," I said.

"No, Lisa. I don't think it will, especially since you

and Sheila are friends."

This was the opening I was looking for, so I took my shot. "Eric, do you think you can stop by?" I asked.

"I don't know, Lisa. I don't think that would be a good idea."

As soon as he said that, I cut him short to not cause more worry. I said, "okay, well I'm going to get going, Eric. I have to take care of some things but thank you for calling to see if we were cool! I will be okay though. Bye, Eric." I ended the call before he could reply.

I thought he would have fallen for that and no sooner than I thought that, my phone rang again, and it was Eric saying he could stop by for a moment.

"Hey handsome, you changed your mind?" I asked.

"Yeah, I can stop by for a minute. I will see you in about 30 minutes," he said.

Okay, that gives me enough time to jump in the shower and put on something comfortable, but sexy. Should I still call Sheila to act like I want to smooth things out with her? I decided I should.

Her phone rang four times before she picked up. I knew she was still pissed because she never lets her phone ring that many times, but I didn't care.

"Hey girl!" I said.

"What do you want, Lisa?" She said angrily.

I kept my cool and didn't feed into the irritation I heard in her voice, I stayed focused on what my plan was. I said, "I was just calling to apologize. I didn't mean anything last night. I was just being my usual flirty self; I know Eric is your man and he cares about you a lot. Plus, our friendship means too much to me for it to be ruined! Besides all those fine men I saw there last night, I had my eye on. I will always need you as my wing-man and you're my girl. I would not want to ever do anything to hurt you!"

I know I have been shady to other females in the past. I may have done my dirt to other females, but I wouldn't even think about going there with her as much as she have done for me. Maybe I was trying to psych myself out by thinking that and knowing I was lying straight through my teeth. But, damn. I wanted Eric.

"Why you were so tense last night? Was there something bothering you, Sheila? You know you can talk to me, girl," I said.

She was still closed off. I could tell she was still feeling skeptical about me by her response, and she had the right to.

"No, I will be okay. It's nothing I can't handle. I'm

just going to relax today and watch my Soul Food episodes that I have on DVD," she said reluctantly.

"Ooooh, girl. I love that show! You're going to have to let me borrow it one day," I said trying to light up the mood.

"Yeah, okay. I will talk to later, Lisa."

"All right. Bye, girl!"

What did she mean by that it was nothing she couldn't handle? Like she had something up her sleeve? I guess I shouldn't be paranoid with the dirt that I was planning on doing. Anyway, I still had 15 minutes to jump in the shower before Eric made it over to my place. Just when the doorbell rang, I was stepping out of the shower and my body was glistening with the water. I threw on my thigh-high bathrobe quickly and let it hang off my shoulders to accentuate my cleavage. I looked through the peephole and saw him standing there patiently waiting for me to open the door. I had my hair pinned up to draw attention to my neck showing even more skin. I opened the door and leaned my body up against it with my left leg facing him, so my juicy thick hip was showing on that side. I saw his eyes undressing me before he even responded to me opening the door.

As he snapped out of it, he asked me, "did you forget that I was stopping by!"

"No, I didn't forget. Why did you ask me that Eric?" I asked with a smile.

"Well, I didn't expect you to come to the door in your bathrobe, looking like you just got straight out of the shower," he said.

"That's because I did just get out the shower, I thought I had enough time before you showed up! Come in, I didn't think you were going to arrive so quickly," I said knowing exactly what I was I doing.

I continued to stand in the doorway, so when he walked past me his body would brush up against mine.

"Make yourself comfortable while I go put some clothes on," I said.

He was sitting on my sofa when I made it back into the living room. Now, this sofa was big enough for two people to fully lay down, which I was hoping I could get him in that position. Maybe I could feel those strong hands gripping my ass and caressing my hips, while his sensual lips are on my tits. The question was, would he fall for my seduction?

A woman knows what she is working with, what clothes, and lingerie items accentuates her bodies' best assets. I had my shortest athletic shorts on, the ones that look like they were from 1976 with the little white strip up the side. They hugged my ass just right and it showed my cheeks. Underneath, I had on my lacy black thong. Also, I had on my white baby tee, because it had deep v cut in the front that showed off my cleavage. Making sure my skin was nice and supple, I had put on my Johnson's lavender baby oil gel. I had on some cute slouchy tube socks.

I sat down right next to him on the sofa and shifted my body sideways, bending my knees towards him. I placed my left arm on the cushion positioned around the back of his neck. He didn't move or seem uneasy. So far so good! I started to play with the buttons on his shirt as I began to talk.

"I'm glad you were able to swing by. I can't stop thinking about you, Eric!" I said.

"Now, Lisa. You know I didn't come over here for that," he said as he gently grabbed my hand removing it from his shirt.

I knew he was curious about me because he smoothly patted my thigh and left his hand there momentarily before moving it. While looking me straight in my eyes, he asked, "Lisa is there something that you are not telling me?"

Out of pure frustration since I didn't reply, he pushed me away and stood up to walk away while saying, "at least that is the feeling I am getting in the pit of my stomach, Lisa! You know more than you are saying, I am really getting pissed off about this whole situation."

As he was reaching for the door, I stopped him. "Hold on, Eric. Okay, dammit your right! I am withholding information from you and I am so sorry because you deserve better. You really do."

I grabbed his arm hoping he would release the door handle, with his back facing he continued tightly grip the door handle. He didn't open it. Then, I knew he was contemplating staying longer than he had planned. I pressed my body up against him, while still holding his arm, and whispered in his ear, "I told you, you deserved better."

He released the door handle and I led him back to the sofa. He sat down leaning back on the couch with his hands on his head, I took my chances and climbed on top of him. I felt his heart rate increase and breathing quickened as he placed his hands around my waist shaking me, I felt his grip tighten.

"Lisa, tell me what you know!" He said.

To keep him on the hook, I fed him what he wanted to hear. What he was thinking Sheila was doing behind his back, even though I knew she was loyal to him. I knew he was thinking she wasn't.

"Eric, now before I tell you this, you have to

promise that you are not going to go to her with this. Do you promise?" I said.

"Yes, yes. Lisa, I promise," he said.

"Well, I don't know how true it is. But, she has told me her ex has been coming back around trying to push his way back into her life! She also said that she had to work out her feelings towards him," I said.

I knew she could not stand Kenny and didn't want anything to do with him. I knew she was really protecting Eric and she wanted a future with him. He was not going to hear those sweet words from me, that the women he loves wants a future with him. Instead I embraced his face with my hands and leaned forward gently kissing his neck, telling him everything was going to be okay. Maybe it was not meant for him and Sheila to be together?

His strength had to be magnified by his anger, because he lifted me up laying me on my backside. I wasted no time wrapping my legs around his waist as his hands explored my body. I moaned as his hands controlled the movement of my body, feeling his firm clasp caress the length of legs, and his lips place sweet kisses across my breast. The kisses were like he was apologizing from being away from my body for so long even though this was our first encounter. I didn't realize he could be so affectionate. He was kissing me so eagerly. All of sudden, he pushed back looking at me with an expression of disappointment.

He vigorously pushed me away, standing up. He was infuriated.

"What the FUCK am I doing? I love Sheila! I have to get out of here, I should have known better! I don't know if I can really trust you, Lisa. You say you are her friend, but here you are laying all your cookies out on the table acting like a desperate SLUT."

"Who the FUCK are you calling a SLUT?! With your sorry ass, you can't even keep your relationship in line. So, even if you think about going to Sheila about what I told you, I will tell her about what happened here today."

He lunged at me, shaking me saying, "you DIRTY LITTLE BITCH! I am not threatened by you in any way."

"You should be more worried about me and what would happen to you if you opened your filthy mouth," I said.

As he headed for the door, he reassured me I was the one that should be worried, because now he knew where I lived.

"I know a lot of people, Lisa. So I would think wisely before making any moves, if I were you. Don't be a stupid SLUT your whole life," he said smirking as he walked out the door.

I was so pissed off at what just transpired, I couldn't even speak the tears just rolled down my face. I'm tired of holding in the mistreatment of men that come into my life, or shall I say that I have invited into my life. I have to bear the burden of my actions. I have brought this behavior towards me like a magnet. I have always heard the phrase, "you accept what you think you are worth," and it couldn't be truer for me.

As the tears continue to roll down my face, I just curled up on the couch in the dark knowing I could never mention this to Sheila! Not because of what Eric said, but because she didn't deserve this type of pain. I knew Eric was not attracted to me in any way, and that his actions reflected his own pain of loving Sheila and having a bleak view of the truth.

17 Kim Shavers

I decided to give Michelle a call, since I was up early getting ready for church. She was weighing heavy on my heart, I also had to go pick up Kyle on the way.

"Michelle! Hey, girl. Either you're really tired from last night or you didn't even come home. Whichever one, give me a call and let me know what's up? All right, talk to you later!"

I know she probably was with Jeremy last night, but it is about time my girl spent some real quality time with him. Memories hold a special place in your life, they can either be dark or bright, but some of them you just can't let go! That day will always hold a memory.

We normally always return each other's calls as soon as we can, but this time I didn't receive a call from her until Kyle and I got out of church.

"Kim, that was a great sermon today, baby!" He said.

"Yes, it was! The preacher always knows what to talk about. Today, it was exactly what I needed to hear. I'm going to let Michelle know about today's sermon because she probably needs to hear it. **Ephesians 5:6** 'let no one deceive you with empty words, for because of these things the wrath of God comes upon the sons of disobedience.'""You're right, baby." "You can always see things the way you want to see them, especially if you don't want to face the truth. That is where people get hurt, when they know the truth deep down inside, but they don't want to face it so they see and hear what they want too, and that can be a dangerous combination. There is something I have been contemplating telling you about Michelle." I said, adding, "now, don't look at me strange, because when she told me I did the same to her and I know it didn't make her feel good. I know I was wrong, but I was very supportive to what I felt she was struggling with. If I recall correctly, it was either the day of or before her party and she said she wanted to talk to me. I was hoping and praying she wasn't going to tell me she was sick, or her mom was sick. It was something I never would have expected to come out of her mouth in my wildest dreams." With high anticipation, Kyle blurted out, "what is it? What happened?" "On that day, she told me that she was hearing voices!" I exclaimed. "Voices?" "Yes, voices. Now, she said it was not a voice with ominous intent." I shuddered. With a look of concern and fear on his face, Kyle asked, "well, did she tell you what the voice said to her?" "Yes, she did," I responded fidgeting before I went further. "She said she was woken up out of her sleep by the voice saying, 'I'm so cold, it's dark in here!' She also said things have been moved, as well as hearing the laughter of a small child." "Kim, I can't believe what I am hearing. What is after her? Did she check the history of her place to see who lived there before her?" "That is the same thing I said. I don't think she did anything like that. I know she would tell me if she was expecting a child, at least I hope she would!" My phone finally buzzed, it was Michelle. "Hello!" She said. "Hey, party animal! How was your evening? You had me worried for a second?" "Why is that?" She asked. "Well, you know we usually call each other back in a reasonable amount of time?" "You are right. I am sorry! Last night was amazing, you won't believe the night I had!" She exclaimed. "Ooooooh, that sounds juicy. How about we meet up later for dinner? You can tell me all about it and I can let you know about today's sermon?" I asked. "Okay! What else is on your agenda for today, Kim?" She asked. "Well, right now Kyle and I are going to have some lunch and then go relax until I meet up with you later," I said. "All right, you enjoy your lunch and I will see you later. Be safe out there." "All right! Will do, bye," I said. I looked over at Kyle, and said, "it sounds like your boy and Michelle are getting close? If he is such a good guy, why do I feel so uneasy? I want to be happy for her, but I don't know what this feeling is." "Really, what did she say? Kim, you know you have the spirit of discernment. I think that came from your mother and grandmother raising you in the church," he laughed. "I'm just worried for her. She really didn't say much, except that she had an amazing evening." "She must have really liked the Camelot Hotel," he said with a smirk. "That's where he took her? I heard that place was stunning, and I guess it would be for a five-star Hotel. I can't wait until dinner tonight! Do you think that he is too good to be true? Look past him being your friend, look at who he is!" Thinking back, I wish I would have pushed further to help her, although sometimes there is nothing that could be done. I said, "For now, where would you like to have lunch Mr. Walters?""We can head over to a buffet place. I can feed you some ice cream," he said. "Don't start being naughty," I said laughing. "Do you remember when we first started dating, Kim? We would watch movie marathons at my place and tear up some ice cream all night?" He asked. "Yeah, baby, I remember. That ice cream went straight to my hips of mine, that is why I had to keep my workout up. That also was before a lot of things started taking off for us in our careers. I could never thank you enough for how supportive you are." "We should make time for little things like that again," he said with a smile. "Well, Mr. Walters, I absolutely would love that. I think that should be arranged," I said.At dinner, Michelle had a glow to her. I had to tell her. "Hey, girl. Look at you, your glowing! Thank you for meeting me for dinner! I hope you are not falling in love with this man already," I laughed. She looked at me coyishly. Right then and there, I knew she was hooked. "Let's have a seat, that way you can tell me more about Jeremy," I said. I watched her every movement and eagerly listened to every word she said. I remember her going on and on about the evening, and how extravagant the room was. She was very detailed about their first sexual encounter. When that was explained, I knew there was no pulling her away from him. Besides, I didn't want her to think that I was against her finding love. Again, I should have pushed harder to be a better friend. I never asked her what made her love him so much. I was thrown off by the next thing she said too. It wasn't so much of what she said it was more of what she said she saw! Later at home, I called Kyle."Hey honey, I know I just dropped you off not too long ago. Can you come stay the night with me?" I asked. "Sure, babe. What's wrong?" "I'm kind of freaked out…" I shuddered. "What are you freaked out about Kim?" He asked."It was when we went to dinner…

Michelle told me that when they checked out she was standing at the counter with Jeremy. She said in the corner of her eye she saw a child sitting in a chair in the lobby, he could not have been older than three or four years old. He smiled at her, but he didn't move. When Jeremy called her name to ask if she was ready to go, she turned away from the child. By the time they headed past the lobby to the front doors, the child was gone." "That is kind of eerie, Kim. What do you think all of this means? The voices, the laughter, items moving, and now she says she saw a small child alone in the lobby of the hotel! We need to pray for her. I am on my way over!" He said.Fifteen minutes later, I heard a knock on my door. It was Kyle, thank goodness!"Thank you for getting here so fast!""Kim, look babe. How do you know if she is telling you everything that has happened so far? You have been friends since college, right?" He asked. "Yes, but what is your point, babe?" "I'm always here. If you say you should do more, and that is how you truly feel, you should tell her when you get that gut feeling. You should tell before it is too late to help her!" He said. "You're right, babe." They have been together for a while now, I should dig a little deeper... *18 Jeremy Stone*

I was heading over to Lisa's house. What the hell am I doing? I could have had her trifling ass meet me at a bar somewhere, especially after the confrontation I saw last night between her and Sheila. I tried to call Shelia after I left Michelle, but she didn't pick up. I hope she is cool. She is probably tired of all this shit that is going on, whatever the truth may be. While I was continuing to have second thoughts, it was then my phone rang, and it was Lisa. Was this a sign?

"Hello, hey Jeremy! You finding your way okay?" She asked.

"Yeah, I will be there in a minute!" I said. I ignored my gut that was saying I shouldn't go. I found out later that Eric had just left her place 10 minutes before I made it over there. She tried her luck with him and lost!

She sweetly responded, "okay, I will see you soon."

I wasn't actually too far away when she called. I

was right around the corner and when I pulled up to her apartment I saw her in the upstairs window motioning and that is when I knew it was about to be trouble, so I had to keep my manly composure and not give in to how fine Lisa is!

"Hi, Jeremy! Come on in, thanks again for coming over! You can have a seat, would you like something to drink?"

"Yeah what do you have?" I asked.

She replied by saying, "oh, I have some green tea, cranberry juice, water, and Mikes Hard Ice Lemonade." She had the sexiest tone, while standing in front of me with her legs spread apart showing skin.

"I will take some cranberry juice with ice if you don't mind."

"Sure, that's fine."

All I kept thinking about was Sheila and how I wish she would just tell me what she was going through. At the party last night, I told her that I trust her and she did promise she would tell me, or at least this is what I keep telling myself.

"Okay, here you go. You got here kind of fast so I'm going to go change, the remote is right there on the coffee table if you want to change the channel."

I was hoping this girl did not come out in close to nothing, because I was going through too much to sustain myself right now! I went ahead and began to turn the channel. While I waited for Lisa to get dressed, I hope what she has to tell me is going to be useful. I ended up leaving the channel on Showtime that had on the Bourne Identity. As I laid the remote back down on the table, Lisa walked up to me with some thong flip flops on, some black stretch pants and a black spaghetti strap tank on. As I mentioned before Lisa was stacked, so I tried my best to stay focused on the issue at hand.

She sat down next to me and put her hand on my leg. She looked me in the eyes and said, "I don't know where to begin, or how tell you what is going on with Sheila, because she is my best friend. I don't want to feel like I am betraying her!"

This girl was good at trying to play the damsel in distress, but it was quite transparent on what she was trying to do.

"Lisa, if there is anything that you need to tell me about Sheila, I think it would be in her best interest if you did. Don't worry about if she is going to be mad at you," I said.

As soon as I said that, tears started forming in her eyes. While she looked away, I gently turned her face back towards mine wiped her tears and quietly asked her, "what is the problem, Lisa? why are you crying? Is Sheila in any type of trouble that I need to know about?"

"Well, I have known you as long as you and Michelle have been going out. I have known about the ups and downs you guys have went through…" She hesitated.

"Lisa, I'm not here to talk about me and Michelle! I'm here to help Sheila if she is in trouble, because my boy Eric is in love with her."

She rolled her eyes when I said that. I just went ahead and asked her if Sheila was seeing someone else?

"Jeremy, I'm sorry. I didn't want you to find out like this." She said.

"Find out what?" I said as I stood up with frustration, looking down at Lisa.

"She promised me that she was going to completely take care of everything without involving Eric," Lisa said.

"What do you mean Involving Eric? Is it someone I know that is keeping her attention?" I asked.

"No, Jeremy. Listen, I think you should just move on and not worry about helping Eric, because obviously she has."

Lisa leaned into me. I leaned back and she began to rub the back of my neck.

"Oh, Lisa. That feels good, I needed that."

"Well Jeremy, let me give you something else you need!" She climbed on top of me and began to kiss me. Her hands roamed down to my belt buckle to unfasten it. I couldn't stop myself, my hands began to roam up and down her thighs and up to her breast. I pulled down the straps on her tank and started to suck on her breast. I then picked her up and laid her down on her back as I positioned myself in between her legs as my hands continued to roam.

I was consumed in the moment. My phone rang, pushing me out of the heat of the moment, it was Michelle. I was in disbelief. Reality came back to me. I sat up and zipped up my pants and looked at Lisa. I said, "what am I doing? You know what Lisa; how do I know that you aren't being your trifling old self?"

I have heard the stories about Lisa from Michelle. It looks like I will have to get the information I need myself.

"You know what, Jeremy. You could have had this any way you wanted it, but you are stuck on trying to get some information on a female that won't even tell her man about her child, and his baby daddy that has been coming down to her apartment and staying almost every weekend," I told him as I fixed my clothes. I stood up in his face.

"When are you going stop being so blind and realize that she has been playing him this whole time," she said.

She finally cracked and gave me the info I needed to help Eric.

"Come on, Jeremy. Look at your boy, Eric. He is financially set, and I know he has given her money more times than once. She has been using him," she said.

It has to be more to it than that. Why has she been trying to protect Eric by not telling him about her child or her child's father?

"I can't believe I almost wasted my time of being over here with you just to get some information out of you. Yeah, you heard me right, so there is no need to look surprised. I had you pegged from the beginning. All a man has to do is show some interest in you and you will drop those panties. What happened here today speaks for itself," I said.

As I headed towards the door, Lisa said something that made me want to throw her through the damn wall.

"Oh, Jeremy. Don't you worry about Michelle, because I will call her to let her know you were over here. I'll tell her the real reason why you didn't answer your phone," she said.

I stormed back over to her and pushed her up

against the wall and said, "I don't think you're going to be saying anything to anybody, because she already thinks you have been trying to push up on me. You try to run up on everybody's man and don't play me for a dummy, Lisa. Whatever you've planned isn't going to work."

I made sure I had my jacket before I walked out of her front door.

Lisa Maxton

As I stood there against the wall, I smiled. Jeremy doesn't know what I have up my sleeve. As I picked up the phone to call Kenny.

"Hello, Kenny?" I said.

"Lisa, damn girl. What's up? I was sleeping."

"Where are you at?" I asked.

"I told your ass I was still here in town laying low, what's going on? Why do you sound so frantic?" Kenny asked.

"Sheila told me that she was going to take Micah somewhere you couldn't find him. She told you that she needed time to think, so you would go away for that reason," I said.

Even though all of that was a lie, I expected more of a reaction. Kenny didn't respond. He just hung up! A voice in the back of my head was telling me I was taking this too far, someone was going to get hurt! But, I ignored it.

19 Michelle Sullivan

"Jeremy, last night was so lovely. I was wondering if we could carry it on over into dinner tonight with our friends. Kim wanted to go out for dinner, but I thought it would be the perfect opportunity for us to have our cook off," I said.

He pulled me close, and said, "well, Miss. Sullivan, that sounds great. I would love to win this competition with my spicy chicken wraps."

I jumped on top of him laughing, "oh, you think so, do you? Well, we will see how that stands up to my homemade spaghetti and meatballs."

I'm hoping this will be a good time to tell him how I feel and how far I want to go with him. I just hope he feels the same now that we have some time in. This is how he makes me feel in my heart, he brings out my creative side. I wanted to show him a little poem I wrote, he has no idea. It is called Blushes.

He places a lily in my hair as I sit under the tree in the cool breeze.
And softly speaks, sweet lady I love that you're real, as rubs the side of my face. His head relaxes on my thigh as he embraces my waist. That tender touch sends me blushes of a 12-year-old girl with a crush.
Afraid he won't be able to handle what I have to give,

letting me hold his heart is what he fears.
Can I share everything with you?
That's here with me and how I always miss
you,
when I lay awake at night thinking of you
my feelings are here, but there is no rush.
Being with you and what we have is precious
enough,
but when my blushes turn to crushes, and my
crushes turn to you.
Will you turn the knob and step right through?
Because I'm not afraid of holding you when you
need me there,
I'm not afraid of listening when you need my
ear.
I'm not afraid of loving you, because loving you
wouldn't be hard to do.

On the ride home, I was glowing like it was the first time we were together. He has continued to show me how special I am to him, but I will come to find out that it's only as long as I stay in the square that he has set for me. Jeremy has hit the target on the bull's eye. I was on cloud nine. We have been talking and dating a month now, so it was about time we moved forward. Where did the time go?

When Jeremy dropped me off at home, he walked me to my door kissed me on my cheek and smiled, and said, "I'll see you later for dinner."

I smiled back and looked him in the eye, and said, "you just make sure you bring you're A-game, Mr. Stone. Be careful going home. Talk to you later!"

When I went in the house, I changed into one of my comfortable jogging suits with the matching top, so I could run to the grocery store to get all the ingredients I needed for my knockout spaghetti. While on my way to the store, I called my girl Kim, to let her know about the change of plans. Kim's phone only rang once before it went to her voicemail, so either she was on it or her battery was low. Being Saturday, I knew the store was going to be packed and it was already going on 4:00 pm. I got in and out with what I needed and just like clockwork, as I was driving home, Kim called me!

"Hello! Hey girl, what's going on?" She asked.

"There has been a change in plans, instead of us going out to dinner we are going to have a little cook competition with Jeremy and I," I said.

"Have you tried his cooking? I mean you two have been together for a while now you should know by now."

"Yes, that it true. But, we either always go out or I would cook every now and then. Although he says he can cook, we will see tonight. Which leaves me only two hours to get ready. So, tell Kyle to have his appetite ready for some good food," I said with a laugh.

"I will. What are you going to make?" She asked.

"Well, I am going to make my momma's famous Spaghetti and Italian Sausage. He said he is going to make some spicy chicken wraps," I said.

"I don't know. He might be in trouble especially if your Spaghetti is going to taste like your mom's. I used to love going home with you on some of the college weekends and your mom had her spaghetti made. It was so good. Michelle, you know Kyle likes spicy food though. I see your guys' strategy. You're making what I like, and he is making what Kyle likes. You guys think your slick, but anyway I will see you around 6:00 pm or a little after," Kim said.

"All right, girl. See you then."

As soon as I made it home, I called Jeremy to see if he was on his way over because he said he was going to make his dish over here.

"Hey, sweetie!" I said.

"Hey, Miss. Sullivan, you really sure you want to do this?" He laughed.

"Of course, you just make sure you bring all of your ingredients over here. Okay, Mr. Stone?" I asked.

"Will do! I will see you in about 20 minutes."

"Okay, see you then," I said.

While waiting on Jeremy to get here, I started on my Italian Sausage. Then, I began to chop up some green peppers and onions to mix in with the sauce for the noodles. Making spaghetti did not take long to prepare, so while I had the sausage cooking on a medium fire, I began to make my secret weapon. My famous Red Velvet cake. Everything was coming together I went into the dining room to set the table.

I did not have a huge house like Kim, but I would say I am pretty happy with my house. I decided to have the table set up as a self-serve type deal. First I put a burnt orange runner down the middle of the table because my table was a dark brown and my accent wall was similar to the runner. Anyway, while I was doing that, Jeremy rang the doorbell and had groceries in hand.

"Hi, you are looking handsome this evening!" I said.

"Why thank you, Michelle. You look lovely as well with your peach dress, but flattering me is not going to help you win," he said laughing.

"Whatever, you know where the kitchen is, so you can go get busy," I said smiling.

"Damn! Every time I come over here, I love looking

at the skylights in your place. Babe, it never gets old. Now that I am done admiring the skylights for the millionth time." He said laughing, "let me create my masterpiece."

Jeremy and I talked about just general things, as we finished preparing our meals. He was in such a good mood. I felt like it would be a perfect night to talk to him. Just as we finished setting the dishes out on the table, Kim and Kyle were arriving.

I took off my apron and went to answer the door, "hey, Kim."

"Hey, Michelle. Can you turn that down?" She asked.

Turn what down? I thought she was talking about me playing Jill Scott, but it was not even all that loud.

"You're beaming and it is hurting my eyes," she said laughing. "He must have whipped it on you last night, girl. I know it's not the first time." In the background, I could hear the exchange between Kyle and Jeremy.

"Hey, Kyle. What is going on?" Jeremy asked.

"Nothing much. I am just ready to enjoy all this nice cooking you two prepared. Oh I heard about the evening you two had. Yeah, man. I see you smiling you continue to treat her like a queen," Kyle said.

"Of course," Jeremy said, whispering. "You know me as long as she stays in her place," with devilish smile on his face. Jeremy shrugged it off and led Kyle into the other room. "Man, come on. Let's get the wine, while the ladies change the music."

"So, Michelle, was it what you expected?" Kim asked.

"Girl, yes! I don't want to get into any details, but when we are together it is different every time. It is like a continuation of exploring my body, girl. His body calls my name," I said with a laugh.

Kim got all excited and started screaming, "shhhh, girl. Come on, let's go eat," I said trying to cut her off.

Kyle took the initiative to say prayer before we sat down to eat. Everything was all set. None of us really talked about work, we were enjoying the food and the music too much to bring work into the mix.

"Wow, Michelle. That Spaghetti was the bomb, girl. How did you learn to make such a great meal?" Kyle asked.

"Thank you, Kyle! I learned to make it from my mom. It was her dish."

While I answered Kyle, I looked over at Jeremy and smiled to let him know that I had this in the bag because he did not know I had a secret weapon. It was vice versa,

178

because Kim liked Jeremy's dish very well. But I had red velvet cake that I also whipped up, all I had to do was put the French white icing on top. I brought everyone a plate out on one of my serving trays.

Kyle stood up and said, "okay, I think we have a winner here." As he puts the last piece of his cake in his mouth.

"Now both dishes were amazing, but this cake just melts in your mouth. So, the winner by dessert is Michelle." Kyle announced.

Jeremy stood up and told me congratulations as he gave me a hug. "The cake was amazing Michelle, and I think we all would enjoy another piece," Jeremy said.

"Sure, you guys are more than welcome to have some more."

Kyle and Kim took their dessert to go.

"Michelle, I had such a lovely time. I am going to enjoy this other piece of cake, but anyway I will call you later!" Kim said.

"All right, girl. Thanks for coming."

"You guys be safe driving home," Jeremy added.

"We will, Jeremy. Bye," Kyle said.

When I got back upstairs, Jeremy was sitting on the couch and there was one piece of cake on a plate in front of him on the coffee table. I walked over and sat down next to him, "babe, I want to talk to you."

When I said that, he turned his body towards me giving me his undivided attention. "What do you want to talk about Michelle?"

For a man that I found to be so sweet to me, somehow there was something about him that was so intimidating, still after all this time we have spent together.

"I never thought I would meet a man like you, Jeremy. You make me feel complete and I love you! I love you, too, Michelle. But where is all of this coming from?" He asked.

"I want us to be together for good. I don't see myself being with anyone else and we are going to have another edition to this beautiful connection we have. I think it will just make things stronger between us." I waited for his reply.

As we sat in silence, I could not read his body language. I had a look on my face of happiness, confusion, and fear all wrapped up into one.

Before he responded, I could tell his mind was racing he had shifted his body away from me. I put my hand gently on his knee and said, "Jeremy, are you okay? Did you hear what I said?"

Dryly, he responded and said, "yes, I heard what you said. What do you expect me to say? I really hope you don't expect me to be happy about this, do you?"

I looked at him with total astonishment. It was like he was a completely different person. I was afraid to say anything else until he asked me another question, it was something in his eyes that was different from before.

"I was hoping you would be happy and wanted the same thing I did," I shuddered.

"Well you thought wrong! I can't believe you, Michelle. How far along, are you?" He asked.

I hesitantly responded saying I am 4 weeks, and I was perplexed because I didn't understand why he was so angry.

He gave me a choice before he stood up to leave with his fist balled up. He spoke with his back to me he wouldn't even look at me!

"You either get rid of it or you put it up for adoption. Either way if you decide to keep it, you won't have me in your life anymore. This is the only time I am going to say this to you. So, the decision is yours."

That was the last thing he said to me before grabbing his jacket and heading down the stairs before I heard the door slam shut. As tears rolled down my face, my body started to tremble because I was a ball of emotions. Maybe he is just scared and maybe he would change his mind because he loves me? I still had a little time to make up my mind before making a big decision like that. I couldn't move. Honestly, I didn't think I was ever going to see him again. After tonight, the voices, the visions, and misplacement of items were going to get worse.

20 Shelia Petty

After Kenny broke into my car and the shit went
down at Michelle's party, something was telling me that
I needed to go check in on my Mom and Micah. I was
getting a gut feeling that something bad was going to
happen! I am already dealing with so much in my life, and
I would never be able to deal if anything happened to mom
or Micah. I would go crazy. Knowing Lisa, she probably
thinks my mom is still in Michigan. My mom was going to
move back to North Carolina where she was born, and she
suggested to take Micah with her. I fought against the idea
at the time, but she has been there for a little while now.
My mom always told me that Kenny was not good for me
and how he would drag me down until I was nothing! With
my mother being the way that she is, she just prayed for
the best outcome for me. Eventually, I woke up and now I
have to deal with the consequences of my actions. The only
good thing that has come out of this is precious son, Micah.

Eric was blowing up my phone. I need to answer
this call, but I didn't have time to talk to him. He kept
leaving me messages saying give him a call. I had my
things packed and in my car. I was ready to go. I asked
the Lord to give me safe travels. I know I owed Eric an
explanation, and I keep telling myself he deserves to know
what was going on.

It was about an 11-hour drive, I know I might have

to stop after eight hours in, but I was prepared to stay for a couple of days once I made it. I don't know why I felt I should call Lisa after the short conversation we had the other day. My heart is telling me that there was something she was not telling me, and I hope the truth will come out!

Her phone rang about three times before she picked up.

"Hello, Lisa. It's Sheila!" I said.

"Oh, hey girl! What's up?" She asked.

"Nothing much, I was just calling to see what you were up to. I know I was a little short with you the las time we talked—"

"I know—hold on, Sheila. I got someone on the other line… Okay. Kenny? Kenny, damn he probably hung up," Lisa said. I don't think she realized that she did not click all the way over and that she still was talking to me.

I knew this whore was up to something, but I played it cool. I was going to act like I didn't hear anything, when she said, "I'm back on the line, so what were you saying?"

"Nothing serious. I just wanted to let you know that we are cool. I don't have any beef with you no more," I said.

"Okay, whatever!" She said nonchalantly. "So, what

are you up to today?"

"Not too much really. I might head out to the mall later. But listen, we can have lunch or something next week."

"Okay! Bye, Sheila." Lisa said.

I called Eric back after I heard that Kenny called her. I definitely knew something was up. Eric's phone went straight to voicemail, so either he was calling around looking for me or he was in a dead zone. Either way I left a message of urgency telling him to meet me at the park where we had our first picnic.

As I sat and waited, my mind was racing I wondered why she was talking to Kenny. I wouldn't put it past her trifling ass if she has been telling him all my business, because she was always on his jock back in the day! I called my mom to let her know I was on my way, but I was going to meet up with Eric first and little did I know he would end up coming with me. I explained to her to why I was coming down, but I did not go into too much detail because I did not want to scare her.

"Sweetie, I want you to be careful. Call me every couple of hours to let me know how far you are. We will talk some more when you get here," my mom said.

"Yes ma'am!"

I don't know when Eric got the message, but he arrived at the park fairly quickly. When he saw me all he could do was hug me and he held me so tight like it was the last time he was going to see me.

"Eric. Baby, please sit down I don't have much time to talk, but I love you and you deserve to know the truth."

The look on his face was of pure expectancy as if he prepared himself for this very moment. I gave him my complete attention down to my body language, I faced him full intent of facing whatever happens after I tell him everything.

"Eric, baby, you are a good man and I want to sincerely apologize to you for keeping you in the dark for all this time. I appreciate you sticking by my side through all of this…" I said.

"What, Sheila baby, your scaring me now. Let me know what is going on because if you are in any type of trouble, I am here for you regardless." He squeezed my hand in reassurance.

As the tears welded up in my eyes, I tried the hardest to keep my composure. I told him about my son, my heart whom I was even afraid to mention, because of my ex. I explained to Eric about Kenny popping up at my apartment late at night and how he stalked me at work.

"I wanted to tell you all of this way sooner, but I did not want you to be at risk of getting hurt by Kenny. He has proven that he no ill regard for human life," I said.

"Sheila, listen, I understand. I am so glad that you finally told me what you have been keeping from me. Regardless of how crazy this Kenny is, I would have not backed down from the situation especially if it has anything to do with you. Where is your son now?" He asked.

"He is safe. He is in North Carolina with my mother. That is the main reason I wanted to urgently meet you because I am heading down there today," I said.

"Don't fight me on this, Sheila, but I'm going with you and that's that! If we have to end up uprooting our lives to the south, then that is what we will do. I love you that much!" He said.

I did exactly what he said and did not fight him on his decision to support me in all of this. I was deeply grateful that he loved me this much and it truly showed, so we headed out. I usually listen to a lot of R&B or Rap, but this time I popped in a gospel cd from Ty Tribbett. This is going to help ease my soul, because I'm really feeling something heavy weighing on me! The next couple of hours I just drove and prayed like I was taught to do, especially when I am troubled. After the first three or four hours, we switched, and Eric took over driving the rest of the way.

The roads were clear most of the way, so our drive was going by pretty quickly. We were three and a half hours into the drive, when my mom called to check to see where I was.

"Hi, momma." I said.

"How far away are you sweetie?" She said.

I didn't tell her that Eric was with me, but I calmly answered her question and said, "I had been driving for about three and half hours, don't worry I am driving carefully. How is Micah momma?"

"He is fine. I haven't let him know that you were coming. I wanted him to be surprised, he misses you."

"I miss him so much, momma. I will see you later tonight. I love you," I said.

"I love you too, baby. I will see you when you make it here, baby!" She said.

When we arrived, I was tired, and I know Eric was especially tired because he drove the rest of the way. But I was so excited to see my mom and my son, Micah. It has been almost one year since I have seen them. I pulled up to my mom's house and was overwhelmed with relief, and comfort by just looking at her house.

It was a quaint two-story home, all white with a wraparound enclosed porch. I got out of the car and went to grab for my bag, when Micah came busting through the door yelling, "Mommy, mommy!"

I immediately dropped my bag, as he ran and jumped in my arms. I held him so tight as tears of joy ran down my face.

"Oh, sweetie. Momma has missed you so much," I said.

"I missed you too, Momma. I have so much to tell you," he said.

I introduced him to Eric, and he shook his hand like a little gentleman saying it was nice to meet him. I can tell that Micah will like him even though he is young. One thing I know is that Micha has a lot of personality!

"How long will you be here, Momma? Please stay?"

"I will be here a couple of days, baby. But it may be longer, so we have plenty of time. When I looked up from talking to Micah, I saw my mom standing on the front porch with her hair pulled back into a bun. She had on the green flared skirt with little white flowers all over it. Seeing her standing there in the outfit I bought her on her last birthday, filled me with joy. I love my mother dearly and would do anything for her.

Eric reached to grab my bag, but Micah wanted to be momma's big boy and carry it. I watched and smiled as he was dragging my bag up the stairs because he insisted on helping me carry my bag. He is such a little gentleman. I hugged my mom and held her like it was the last time I was going to see her. Eric just watched patiently. As she held me by my arms and just looked at me, and said, "you have to take of yourself, baby. There is a 5-year-old little boy in there that needs you. We can talk later when Micah's in bed, but for now I have some meatloaf, mashed potatoes, and corn in the kitchen if you're hungry.

She looked up at Eric and smiled, and said, "Now who is this handsome, gentlemen that you have brought home with you?"

I coyly laughed and said, "Momma, this is Eric. My boyfriend. We have been together a few years now, and he is very sweet and supportive."

"Nice to meet you, Eric. That is beautiful to hear. He has to be special if he has come all the way down here with you. Come on in the house, so you can eat and rest because I know you are tired after that drive," She said.

"Thank you so much, Mrs. Petty. It is a pleasure to finally meet you!" Eric said.

We will always be her babies. My brother lived here too. My brothers were 19 and 22. The last time we saw our father was when they were 4 and 7. They have been with my mom since, keeping her safe. Also, they never liked Kenny either.

The couple of days I was there went by so fast. I spent a lot of time with Micah and Eric. It was nice to visit with by brothers as well as staying up talking with my mom. It broke my heart to see Micah crying when we drove away. But I knew one day I would come back and stay for good. All I could think about was what my mom said last night. She looked me in my eyes while holding both of my hands, and said, "baby, life is too short for it to be wasted away. You will look up one day and your life has passed you by. A man will test you just to see how far he can push you. Once you have had enough, there will be no more taking from you because by then you would have walked away from the turmoil."

I explained to her about everything that was going on. She didn't want me to leave too. I got home late Tuesday night and I called my mom as soon as I made it. I didn't even bother to listen to any of the messages. I just laid down with Eric. He held me, and we went to sleep. If I knew what was going to happen to me by Thursday, I would have never come back to Michigan!

21 Jeremy Stone

It was the middle of the week already, and it seemed like I was just over Michelle's house Sunday, which was pleasant until she said she wanted to talk. I haven't seen her since she dropped the bomb on me about this baby, bullshit. She was blowing up my phone all day when I walked out on her. I didn't have any empathetic feelings at all for her with her dramatic tears! They could have been sincere, but I was not falling for it. Her saying how much she loved me, and pleading her case on how she was not trying to trap me! She doesn't realize it has nothing to do with being or feeling trapped. It has more to do with not bringing a child into this dark world. If she can't figure that out, she is a dense female. My day couldn't get any more hectic thinking about this and my past. When I was informed Eric was in the lobby, I completely forgot he was stopping by. I haven't spoken to him since Michelle's party.

So, you can imagine my sarcastic enthusiasm, when my receptionist, buzzed in saying there is a Mr. Eric Mathews was waiting in the lobby.

I wanted so much to tell Charlene to extremely apologize and reschedule, because I have not had a chance to go over my reports for the day and have I had a chance to speak with Sheila after leaving Lisa's place. I told her to send him back to my office anyway. Little did I know, he had already had an in-depth conversation with Sheila about all the drama going on in her life! He came into my office pacing back and forth.

"Hey, Eric. Man, what's going on?" I asked.

"Jeremy, man. I messed up. I really messed up! I think I completely fucked up things between me and Sheila."

"Calm down, what are you talking about?" I asked.

"Well, first, I went over Lisa's. You know Sheila's friend. She said she wanted to talk to me regarding Sheila, so I can find out some information on why she has been acting so strange these few weeks. I went over Lisa's house and things got heated..." He shuddered.

"What do you mean heated? Did you fuck her?"

"Nah, man. It did not get that far. I did lose myself for a bit, she came out in some really short athletic shorts and one of those baby white tees. One thing led to another and the next thing I know she sat down close to me with her body facing me, showing her thighs, which were screaming for my attention! She started to caress the side of my face gently and told me everything was going to be okay. She said maybe it was not meant for me and Sheila to be together. She was telling me all this shit about some other man and just pissed me off for the moment. We started to make out and stuff. Then, I stopped myself before we went any further. I realized how much of an idiot I was. Now I'm worried that she is going to run her mouth to Sheila although, we are finally at a good place. She told me everything that was going on and we visited her family."

"Wow. All right, man. Listen, I know you love Sheila and all, but it's not like you aren't well deserving of getting some action from another women especially after all the crap Sheila has put you through," I said.

"Anyway, after I stopped Lisa got mad because I told her I was using her for information and I knew what type of slut she was. But, Lisa did tell me about the ex that Shelia was dealing with. Shelia was protecting me from him because he has a history of being dangerous..." Eric said.

"Are you carrying, Eric? Just in case you run into this crazy nigga? If you don't want to go buy nothing from a gun dealer, I got somebody I can hook you up with," I said.

"Damn, J. You get down like that?"

"Look man, just because I'm educated does not mean I don't have street sense."

He had no idea of my past ad how I had to survive before all of this.

"If it gets to that point, I will make sure I reach out

to you," Eric said.

"All right, man. Listen, it is cool everything worked out between you and Sheila. Honestly, I wouldn't worry about Lisa saying a damn thing."

"Why do you say that?" He asked.

I definitely was not about to tell him about my encounter with Lisa, and how I had to threaten her ass too. So, I just told him you know what type of female she is!

"She will try to do anything to stay relevant. She is not going to say shit!" I said, adding, "Hey man, listen, I don't mean to cut our conversation short, but I need to go over these blueprints for tomorrow. We are so close to completing the developmental stage of this project. Let's try and catch up later in the week, maybe grab a beer or something that cool with you?"

"Yeah, man. That would be cool. I really appreciate it, you willing to help me and all." He said.

"No problem, man. You my boy, but I really need to get back to work. I will be in touch!"

Today must not be my day, because the next thing I know Charlene buzzed in telling me that Michelle was on her way back to my office. Now, I told Charlene that she was allowed back to my office without permission, so I couldn't be mad at her. I also I never thought she would be the type of female that would just pop up at my job either, but you could never put anything past anyone. People are capable of anything if they are pushed hard enough! So, I prepared myself to what she possibly had to say, but my main reason for trying to keep calm because I did not want to lose my job.

She walked into my office with the most pitiful look on her face, it's almost like my eyes narrowed onto her stomach. She wasn't starting show yet, but it felt like my mind was playing tricks. At least she was dressed decent. She had on the baby blue jogging suit and a pair of tennis shoes I bought her.

With my jaws tightened I told her sit-down. "What the hell are you doing here Michelle? What the fuck do you want I already told you your choices! You think coming here like this is going to make me change my mind? Michelle, this is my job. You and your melodramatic act is going to have to be cut short today because you should not be here," I said.

Tears started streamed down her face as she started to speak, with her occasionally gasping for air, "Jeremy, I just don't understand why this would make you not love me anymore. I would think that it would make you fall deeper in love with me!"

She looked up at me with deep despair and grabbed

a hold to my pants leg, saying, "I am carrying your child, doesn't that mean anything to you?"

I gripped her hands back, shaking them and not caring if I was hurting her in. I pushed her hands away.

"I want you to touch my stomach!" She said.

"Michelle, the thought of me touching you there sickens me." I shuddered in anger.

As I stood her up pushing her up against the wall with force, I pressed my face close to hers as I spoke with hostility in her ear, and said, "you coming here was the wrong decision. A huge mistake on your part Michelle. Your behavior is pathetic and to think I wanted to marry you! You disgust me right now because I thought you were a strong woman. But, you are weak. Why couldn't you just continue to be obedient and everything would have been fine? You are going to wipe your face and walk out of here as if nothing happened."

Wiping the flowing tears from her face, she seemed to be instantly overcome with a tranquil feeling. She said to me in the softest voice, "Jeremy, I want you in my life and you mean the world to me. I understand what it is that I need to do now!"

Was it cruel giving her false hope, saying I was going to marry her? Yes, it could have been. What she does with what I say is on her and it defines her character, which has nothing to do with me. Like I keep saying, we all have choices. What you do with those choices is up to you. You can't blame anybody but yourself if the choice you made makes a tainted path you are destined to and must walk!

The flame has been lit inside of me and my past was a raging fire illuminating behind me. It was fighting to eat up my future and re-claim what I have fought to forget. The past has reared its ugly head and I just might let it! I watched her exit my office and head down the hallway and the further away she became the more the levels of my energy had started to change. It was as if there was something inside of me controlling my metaphorically switches of emotion. I enjoyed being in control, letting nothing define what the next move in my life was going to be. I knew how to adapt to each environment I was put in. I knew this was not going to be the last time I saw Michelle, while she came up with her choice.

I sat back down at my desk and spun around to face the window, so I could look out at the world. Trying not to go to war with my thoughts, but the reflection on the glass was not of me, but it was of the little boy I used to be. My life was not always this way. I had to learn to define my destiny, although I was not always able to escape my fate as a young boy. I still hear the cries of my restrained memory. I could picture myself curled up in a dark corner as I watched my mother's body lay limp from her drug induced haze in the distance. I have had to sit and watch her be violated sexually by her dealer in order to get her fix.

Momma is sick! She would say. *Bab go sit in the corner, it will only be a moment. This is going to help me get better.*

As I sat there watching her being touched, this stranger revealed himself to me as a monster. Long fingers with pointed nails, a monster with a muscular physique, a demonic facial structure, and the tongue of a lizard lay on top of my mother. He possessed everything she was, but this is not what she saw. She was blinded by the poison of the drugs. When he felt as if there was nothing else, he would consume of her. He turned his attention towards me. This sent me into a dark place to escape what was happening to me. I would zone in on one thing and go to another world. This would happen up until I ran off that one day.

You can hold so many memories to the point where you start to create different areas in your mind, labeling each area to lock away. Or, you try to completely block the out or fill that space with a happier time if you are lucky. As you get older, sometimes you find out that there is no escape.

After all of these years, I don't even know if my mother is still alive. I don't have the desire to know or even care if she is. I continued to stare out at the world and my focus for work was completely gone. I decided to call it a day, I will deal with work later. Before I left my office,

I could see from my window that Michelle was walking to the parking structure where she had parked. I knew she probably was going to call Kim and just bury me in some deep shit, telling her how I have been treating her.

It was the start of my favorite time of year, which was fall. The sun was still shining, while there was a nice breeze blowing. The few trees that were downtown had begun to change colors. It reminded me of this one fond memory that I had as a young boy before everything started to go to shit.

I can remember going camping. The long, soothing ride to get there with the window cracked. As we drove, I saw many different trees with so many different bright colors. There were red, yellow, and orange leaves. I enjoyed how the sun would break through the trees and shine on my face as we drove. I would just close my eyes and smile, while feeling the brightness of the sun staring back at me. This is the one memory I keep locked away to help me escape when that dark cloud called my life comes calling.

I was distracted from my thoughts, when a homeless woman walked up to me asking for some change. This wasn't an uncommon sight working downtown. There were many homeless people, but not enough shelters to hold them all. I stood there staring at her as she rocked back and forth with her hair in a mess all over her head, her lips were dry and crusted. She had on a dingy white sweater that had holes in it with some black faded leggings and some busted flip flops.

Before I handed her the change I had in my pocket, she said, "God Bless you, Son." As I watched her sashay across the street to the boy on the corner, this made me think about my mother. I really didn't have the desire to know if she was alive or dead. This might be a sad thought to most people, but it was a thought of remiss to me!

22 Michelle Sullivan

As I walked out of his office, I put on a brave face. I wiped my tears even though I was broken. I could feel his eyes burning a hole in my back until I was no longer in his eyesight. Not only was my heart broken, but I felt numb inside. I decided to call Kim. I needed to see my friend. I was carrying a blessing. A blessing I was not sure if I was going to keep. I was leaning more towards of making that sacrifice to keep Jeremy in my life. He wanted to marry me. The thought of that excites me more than anything. I have lost myself in him. If we get married and become one, I just know we can re-visit having a child.

Kim didn't pick up, but knew she would call me back, so I left her a message. I tried my hardest not to sound like I was an emotional wreck, but I knew whatever message I left her that she would be able to read between the lines.

"Hey Kim, it's Michelle. I want to go over something with you that I have been thinking about. I need your opinion, call me back so we can meet up," I sighed.

I sat in my car and zoned out, thinking about the man that I held so close to my heart. He meant the world to me, but he showed his true colors when I said I was carrying his child! He spoke the words so bluntly to me "I'm not sure I want kids, and least not with you!"

I was speechless I could not believe what he was saying to me. Here I am finding out I am three weeks along and the man I am head over heels with just ripped my heart out of my chest. I still think that I could change Jeremy by letting him see how amazing it would be to have a child with me. I would soon learn that the more I expressed to him that I wanted a life with him the more he pulled away. Again, I told myself I was not going to lose him, so I put his thoughts before mine.

Kim ended up calling me back by the time I made it home. She spoke with openness. That is what I love about my friend, she is not judgmental. She always knows when something was wrong with me no matter how hard I tried to disguise it.

Before I got out of my car, she was telling me she was on her way over so we could talk. I gave Kim a key to my place a while ago just in case of an emergency. So, by the time she made it over to my place and let herself in, I was curled up on the couch. I was listening to Maxwell. The mood was depressing and that is exactly what she said when she walked in and found me in the dark.

I heard her yelling out my name as she entered the house tripping over my shoes, my jacket, and purse. "Michelle? Michelle? What the hell is going on? Are you okay?"

She sat down next to me on the couch placing her hand on my side, saying, "Michelle, please talk to me tell me what's wrong. Michelle, you are scaring me!"

I couldn't speak at first, I just sat up and laid my head on her lap and the tears that I held back began to flow again.

"Whatever it is sweetie, everything will be okay. I'm glad you called. you don't need to be by yourself right now. Just breathe and when you are ready, tell me what happened."

I took a shaken breath, and said, "you remember the night we did the competition dinner, and the whole night went amazingly well?"

"Yes, I remember I really enjoyed myself."

"Well after you guys left, I told Jeremy I needed to talk to him, and you know we have been together for a little while now. So, the conversation was going well and as we confessed our love for each other. I told him that I wanted no one else in my life but him…"

"Okay, what's wrong with that? That was a beautiful thing to say."

"It wasn't that, that made him fly off the handle. It was when I told him that I was pregnant," I said.

"Aww. Michelle, how far along are you? What did he say?" She asked.

"I am 3 weeks now. I don't know if I am going to keep it after I tell you what he said. He said to me, 'what do you expect me to say? I really hope you don't expect me to be happy about this, do you?' He also gave me an ultimatum."

"What? Wait are you serious? He is being a real asshole about this. I knew something was up with him when you started dating him. I noticed he was always in control of majority of what you guys did. What was the ultimatum?" Kim asked.

"He didn't even look at me when he said this, he stood up to leave with his back to me. He uttered these ugly words: You either get rid of it or you put it up for adoption. Either way if you decide to keep it, you won't have me in your life anymore this is the only time I am going to say this to you," I started to cry harder.

"Michelle, look at me! You are not really pondering over one of his options are you?" Kim asked.

"Honestly I don't know! I'm afraid of losing him. I gave him some space thinking it would change his mind. But, I stopped by his job today and it was worse. It was like he was someone else. It also felt like it triggered something inside him," I said.

"Don't tell me he put his hands on you! This sounds dangerous, Michelle. You really don't know what he is capable of. Maybe what he is showing you right now is who he has been all this time and he just couldn't hide it anymore," she said.

"When I went to his office today, he didn't know I was coming. Before I left his office he forced me up against the wall. He asked me, what the fuck did I want? There was nothing else to be said and he gave me my choices again. He told me I made the wrong decision coming to his office. He said my behavior was pathetic and that I was showing him weakness. He told me he wouldn't consider marrying me now. Kim, he would not even touch my stomach! He told me to wipe my face and walk out of his office as if nothing happened."

"Michelle, I am so sorry you are going through this. I can't believe he said he would marry you. Honestly, he wanted to marry you because he was always in control. There really is no guarantee that he does really want to marry you. He could be telling you that just so you will get rid of the baby. So, who is to say that if you actually do either one of his idiotic choices that you both will be together after that?" She asked.

"Kim, something in my heart is telling me whatever decision I make time will heal the wounds."

"Michelle, I'm telling you that you don't need him. You are worried about losing the wrong thing. This child is a big part of you just as well as it is a part of him. If you decide to either one of those decisions, do you realize what you will be missing out on?" She asked.

"I am still young, Kim. I can always try again! Michelle are you listening to yourself I don't think this man will ever want children. Something obviously has you convinced that he would change over time. Have you ever thought he may not want to have kids with you!"

"Kim! Why would you say something like that? Why would I be losing the wrong thing?" I asked.

"I said it because it's the truth and you are my friend, Michelle. You're like a sister to me, you know that. I would not say anything to you that I felt like wouldn't help you. What you will be losing out on, while you are hoping and waiting that he would come around, will be the connection you will have with that blessing you are carrying. If you abort the baby, wouldn't you ever wonder what it would have been like to hold him or her in your arms for the first time? What it would be like to see the first time he or she opens their eyes? The first time you hear the baby cry. You will never know what any of that will be like if you make that decision! All of this is over a man you are not really sure is actually going to stay if you do this.

"Now if you carry him to term and then give him up, don't you think that would even be worse? You will always wonder where he is, what he likes, if he is being treated right. I know you probably would even think about the fact of if he is being bounced around from foster home to foster home."

"Kim, I wouldn't even allow the nurse let me see him or hear him cry long. I would just have the nurses take the baby straight out of the room after I give birth."

"You still would have a major connection to that child, Michelle. You would have carried him 9 months…"

"The more we talk about this, Kim, the more I am getting stressed out," I said.

"Well, that is one thing you do not need while carrying a child. I do think you should take some time and really think about all of this. I would love to have a little nephew or niece. So, how about I go into your kitchen and make us some popcorn while you find us a movie to watch? It is important that you relax."

I know Kim had her heart set on the fact that she could possibly be an Auntie and I knew she would help me with anything I needed, but I could not let that affect my decision. Kim being there really helped me snap back, we watched a comedy and she stayed until about 8:00 pm, because we both had to get ready for work.

With my thoughts continuing to weigh on me, I went ahead and prepared for the next day with my regular routine. I started running my bath water while I let the dogs out one last time for the evening. They know when they come back in it is time for everyone in the Sullivan house to wind down. I laid out my uniform for the next day before getting in the tub, wherever I went there was Roxi and Tango. They laid right in front the bathroom door. It seemed like as soon as I crawled into bed and closed my eyes, my alarm was going off. I don't know if I can consider that a good night sleep or just to be prepared for what was in store for me today! I went ahead and dragged myself out of bed jumped in the shower got prepared and headed out of the door. I don't know how I was running late especially when my alarm clock went off on time. Today was going to be crazy, even the dogs were acting crazy this morning and that's not like them. I don't know what it was, but I had to get to work.

Just when I started to wish Jeremy would love me unconditionally like Eric loves Sheila, that's when I saw him. Jeremy was across the street with another woman. I was so tired of thinking I have finally found someone, then they turn around and leave me in the dirt! It took everything I had not to walk through traffic to get across the street and slap the crap out of him, especially after how he treated me

in his office. Has he moved on already? I was furious as
I watched him rub the woman's hand in a consoling way.
I couldn't focus on this I had to get to work. I know one
thing my mind was made upon. Why would I want to have
his child; he is clearly showing me that he meant what he
said. I know he didn't expect me to see him, but the truth
always comes out no matter how hard you try to hide it.

On my way into the building, I was blowing up
Kim's phone. But, she didn't answer and that just made
me more pissed off because I could not vent to my best
friend about how much of an ass Jeremy really is. Damn,
she was right! I bet he still will try to come sniffing around
after he gets tired of that trick he was with. I scheduled an
appointment with the doctor for the following week. The
next time this happens it will be the right time, if there is a
next time.

23 *Michelle Sullivan-My Decision*

After making the appointment to abort the baby, it
would come later to me that I was not being true to myself,
knowing that if I did this it would not change anything.
My decision would haunt me! It has been years since I had
the procedure, and I really thought me making that choice
would bring me and Jeremy back together. His words were
proven to be untrue after the baby was aborted.

Jeremy and I ended up speaking after I saw him
with the mysterious lady at the coffee shop. He expressed
to me that I was not the women he wanted to be with. I
felt empty. My heart was in my throat. I never heard from
Jeremy again about my decision. I did what I usually do.
I held my emotions in and continued to work at the hotel.
It was slow that night at the hotel. I covered the front
desk, while I sent my agent to break as I started to pull the
reports.

Before I knew it, I caught myself thinking about
the baby. Even though I felt like it was going to be a boy,
I actually never found out if it was going to be a boy or a
girl. My eyes started to tear up, regretting my decision. I
was still forever connected to my child. The exact thing that
Kim said was going to happen was happening, the racing
thoughts of me wondering what if!

I tried to take my mind off things by writing out

my feelings. Not only were my thoughts on the baby, but my thoughts were manifesting what if Jeremy and I did stay together and had a family together. I am most content when I write. The poem is called Magnetic Chemistry, which is what I thought we had. I was so in love with him!

Magnetic Chemistry

How can I think of you constantly and never pick up the phone? Is it a convenience to the other? You want a taste of my sweet nectar to tide you over until the next fix. You're that blanket of contentment that surrounds me, a magnetic chemistry that should always shield me! The words being in love with you are more than just a feeling that rolls off my tongue. It's a mix of emotions that develops an uneasy reaction of uncertainty. A combination that creates unchartered waters that only you seem to calm. I fight against what was made evidently clear. A magnetic chemistry that's undeniably drawn together. Drawn together from two different directions, what brought this on? Is it meant to be? The depth of my love invested in a distant shore. I want you closer to me. I need you. We are an intertwined piece of art making a beautiful sight. Wrap me up in your arms. I'm yours, waiting on this distant shore. As the sun sets and rises again, I often ask myself, will this magnetic chemistry last?

I called Kim. I instantly regretted it because of late it was. She didn't answer at first, but she ended up calling me right back. When I picked up on the first ring, you could hear the grogginess in her voice.

"Hey, Kim. I am so sorry for calling you so late!" I said.

"Michelle? Michelle, are you okay? Where are you?"

"I am so sorry for waking you up. Yes, I am okay. I'm at work and I am having a hard time tonight. I know it has been a few years since I aborted the baby, but it is really bothering me what I ended up doing!" I said.

"Michelle, I know it is a lot to deal with and I can't imagine what you have been through. I do understand you feel like a huge part of who you is gone, but you will always be connected to that child no matter how old you get. No matter if you have other children! There will always be a piece of you that can't be replaced..." She paused, "Michelle?"

"Yes, I am listening."

"Do you realize what today's date is?"

With a tremble in my voice, I slowly responded to

her and instantly realize what she was going to say, "today is October 21st, which makes it exactly three years since I had the abortion."

"What have you been thinking about, Michelle?" She asked.

"Over the years, this has affected me to the point where I have been needing counseling sessions with my preacher. At the time, I thought it was the right thing to do so I could put Jeremy's needs before mine. At the time, I do admit you telling me all the things I would miss, I dismissed completely. All those things have come back to haunt me. I didn't tell you, but last week I saw Jeremy passing. Although he didn't see me, I didn't draw attention to myself. Seeing him brought everything back to the surface that I have been fighting to let go by going to the counseling sessions," I said.

"Michelle, do you at least feel like the sessions are helping you? Does it help you cope with your decision?" She asked.

"Yes, in a way."

"What do you think it meant when you were hearing childlike voices and seeing that little boy?"

"You know, Kim, that is something that I will never forget. I honestly just think that was a sign, warning me that I was actually going to end up pregnant by Jeremy. It showed me what I could have," I said.

In my mind, that is what I was telling myself. Although, I knew in my gut that it was something deeper than that. Something that still has not yet revealed its true intent to me. Memories from my past that I buried awoken.

"I have never mentioned to anyone until right now what I am about to tell you…"

"Why do you feel you need to tell me, Michelle?" She asked.

"It is eating away at me, Kim! I thought I could keep these feelings buried, but my past has evidently affected my future." I took deep breath and continued, "I always told you that I had two sisters and two brothers growing up, but I actually was supposed to have 3 sisters. She would have been our eldest sister. This is something that I guess I never could escape, because I have just relived my mother's story."

"How so, Michelle?"

"Her presence was always there in the house with us…" I said.

"What do you mean her presence? What happened to her?" Kim asked.

"My mother told this story to my sisters and I to protect us and warn us from what was out there in the world. She wanted us to be aware that there are wolves in sheep's clothing. It was before she had met our father. My mom stayed in her own apartment on the second floor on the Southside of Chicago. It was a crisp fall day when a repair man came into the building, claiming to be an electrician for the apartment management company. So, my mother didn't have any reason to think that this man would cause her any harm. The man came to her door at 10:00 am, introducing himself as Damien. He even showed his employee badge and said that he was here to check the wiring in the kitchen. By this time, most of the people in her building had gone off to work already, and it came to be known that he waited to see how many people left the building before entering." I paused.

"She told us that she let him in and directed him to the kitchen, and she kept her distance watching him do his job as he created casual conversation. She said she had started to get that eerie feeling in her stomach that something was going to go wrong. When he finished, he headed to the front door as if he was about to leave and my mother followed behind him to lock the door. He turned to her and said, 'I forgot take something that I want!' When he said that, my mother said she looked at him in confusion, and as she turned to run to grab anything to protect herself. He hit her in the head, knocking her out. Upon awakening, she said she was lying in the middle of her front room floor. Her dress was raised above her head and her panties were down hanging off one of her ankles. The front door was cracked open," I shuddered.

"Michelle, sweetheart, I had no idea that you were harboring such a horrible story about your mom! How do you feel that connects to you, because you said you were reliving your mother's story?" She asked.

"In the end, my mother ended up getting pregnant from the man who raped her. Although, we came into her life way later we were told that she struggled with the decision to keep that child. Later on, as our mother told us that she had to make the agonizing decision to abort even after she found out what she was having. When she met my father, their relationship grew, and she ended up getting married. That is when we began to come along, as they built a family. That part is not what is important or the significant part of this story, it is what happened after we settled into our home. When little items like our toys were being misplaced, my mom recognized exactly what was happening. I know she was tormented by her decision the rest of her days, even though she kept a brave face for us."

"Kim, again I apologize for calling so late and keeping you up."

"Sis, you never have to apologize, especially when

you are so vexed with your thoughts! I am here to give you whatever advice I can even, if it just lending an ear to listen."

"Let's get together for lunch tomorrow before you go to work," I said.

"Okay. I would love to get some sleep. Love you sis, talk to you soon."

"Love you too."

When I got off the phone with Kim, my employee was returning from their break, so I headed to the back office to finish running the nightly reports. I tried to focus on my job, but my mind kept reverting to a poem that I wrote my mother one Mother's Day.

When I Look at You...........

I couldn't find a card to say what I exactly feel in my heart. You made the sun come out when it was dark. Thoughts I put in the back of my head, places we lived, the things I saw you go through. I would think, how can someone be that strong to find her way in that dark cloud? You did and you had us right there with you. When my trial of life comes, I hope I can be as strong as you. When I would see you cry, I didn't know the reason why? But now, I know you were praying for the Lord to give you determination and patience inside. He made you our protector through situations that you could only make better. He made you our provider when it seemed there was no means. He gave you the courage for all of us when we were scared. You may have been also, but we couldn't tell. When I look at you and the day comes when I have to be a provider, I hope I can be as strong as you. It's been many days that I have seen you with weight on your shoulders, but you would get on your knees and ask the Lord to help you bare though it. When I look at you and my weight comes, I hope I have as much faith as you. To this day, I say to myself, how could you have made it through all those hard time with us on your back? I smile and think you were our provider, our protector, and our courage. You guided us through that dark cloud to the sun. You are our mother.

My shift was close to ending, and I pushed myself to finish my work. As I drove home, it kept playing over and over in my mind. As I face my trial of life, will I be as strong of a woman as you! Will I make it through? I don't know…

24 Michelle Sullivan- My Destiny

The next morning when I made it home from work, I was exhausted. I knew I was supposed to meet up with Kim for lunch. I began to take off my uniform when I noticed on the floor there was a picture halfway showing from under my dresser. I bent down to pick it up and it was a sonogram picture of the baby. I stood there staring at the picture and chills covered my body as a brush of cold air came over me. I knew I had gotten rid of all the pictures. There was no possible way that one was left. I was so tired I just threw the picture on the dresser and was going to throw it away later when I got out of the shower.

I jumped in the shower and just let the hot water run over my body. It felt like everything that I was struggling to deal with was going down the drain. By the time, I got out of the shower the mirror had fogged up from the steam. I leaned over the sink to wipe the mirror clear with my hand. As I looked at myself in the mirror, I didn't recognize my own reflection. It was me I was looking at, but my skin was dry and discolored. The vibrancy of my natural color had turned gray.

I gazed at my face in disbelief of what I was looking at, was this showing me what I was about to face?

I whispered, "Lord, whatever this is I am about to face, please be with me."

I headed back into my bedroom to grab my lotion from my dresser and right where I left the picture, it was gone. I thought it may have been blown on the floor from me having the window cracked. So, I got down on my knees to check and see if it was back under the dresser where I originally found it, but it wasn't there. I looked under the bed maybe to see if it had blown under there, but it was not there either.

I brushed it off. I went ahead and climbed into bed to get some sleep before I had to meet up with Kim for a late lunch. It didn't take me long to fall asleep once my head hit the pillow. As soon as I drifted off to sleep, I started to dream of the Café where I met Jeremy. The only thing different was that I was standing outside of the Café on a beautiful sunny day looking through the window as if I was watching a movie. It was like it was yesterday when we met. Everything was so vivid. I stood there and watched as we conversed.

As I gazed at the memory of what my life used to be in my dream, I saw a reflection of the same little boy that I saw at the Camelot Hotel. He was standing on the sidewalk right behind me. When he appeared, it caused the atmosphere in the dream to change. The sun that was illuminating before, had turned into a cloudy day.

The times that I would see him before he would just sit and stare at me. When I turned around, he just stood there. I took a step towards him to ask him where his mommy was, he smiled stretching his arms towards me as if he wanted me to pick him up. I squatted down to reach out for him when he walked closer towards me. I was about to pick him up when he whispered in my ear with the same eerie childish voice that woke me up a while ago. He said, "I'm cold, it's so dark in here!"

When I heard those words in my ear, I leaned back and looked him in his face. His smile was gone. His eyes had turned a piercing dark grey. Everything began to feel so real as I saw myself in his eyes, I felt my breath being taken away. As I started to gasp for air, he broke away from my hold and ran around the corner. I proceeded to follow him when I hit the bend to the corner, he was nowhere in sight. I woke up gasping for air. My heart was pounding. What I had done had really began to manifest itself in my consciousness, and it was clear there was no escaping the choice I had made.

I looked over at the time and noticed I was going to be late meeting Kim. I rushed to get dressed. When I got in the car, I realized Kim had called me five times. I immediately called her back. I didn't want her heading over to my place because if she felt as if something was wrong, she would. I dialed her number contemplating as it rang if I should tell her about the dream.

"Hello, Michelle? Girl, I was on my way over to

your house. I thought something was wrong."

I kind of shrugged it off with a laugh, saying, "nah, girl. I'm good I am on my way to meet you for lunch."

"Are you sure you are okay? Especially after the phone call I received from you last night, you really have me worried," she said.

"I know, I know. Again, I am sorry I feel there is something that is about to happen in my life that I can't avoid…" I said.

"What do you mean?" She asked.

"We will talk when I get there. I will see you in a little while."

"Okay! Drive safe, Michelle."

I don't know if this was something I should keep from her.

I made it to the restaurant where I was meeting Kim. I still had a few hours before I had to clock in for work, so I was able to really sit back, relax, and enjoy my meal without rushing. As I was walking towards Kim at a back booth in the restaurant, I immediately tried to cover up what I was feeling with being excited to see her. I thought it would work, but she read me like a book when she stood to hug me.

"Hey girl! Have a seat. Have a seat. Uh-oh, what's wrong, Michelle? Why were you late?"

Just when I believed that I had gotten pass dealing with my ghost, I was wrong. I guess I have been trying to psych myself out by continuously telling myself that there was nothing wrong. I gave up on that and told myself that I was going to face whatever was in my future.

"Michelle? Michelle? Snap out of it! What is going on with you?" Kim shook at my arm.

"It's happening again, Kim. The visions, the voices, and now it has started to invade my dreams," I said.

"Your dreams! Really, Michelle, what I can do to help? I am really starting to worry about you. You are always a concern of mine, but now it has been giving me such an uneasy feeling," she said as tears were forming in her eyes.

"Kim, don't cry you're going to make me cry."

"I'm crying because I'm afraid for you. My heart tells me that this is more than you are ready to confront."

As tears started rolling down her face, I began to tear up because I know we have gone over this multiple times before.

"This morning when I made it home, I was so

exhausted so I decided to take a quick shower. I went into my room over by my dresser, and I know you are probably wondering where this going. It happened when I looked down and saw a corner of what I thought was a piece of paper sticking out from up under the dresser. It was one of the sonogram pictures that I had gotten rid of."

Kim asked, "Michelle, are you sure that you got rid of them all? I do remember you telling me you had a moment when you spazzed after aborting the baby and destroyed your room. I know you had a break down because you started to realize what you had let go..."

"During that period, I do admit I did become very angry. I ripped up all the sonogram photos and threw them out after I had calmed down. This picture was completely intact, not put back together. Kim, it looked as if it was just freshly printed and handed to me. I tried not to be too freaked out about what I found so I threw it on the dresser to ignore it. I was looking at myself after the shower and I didn't recognize the person looking back at me!"

I see how Kim was looking at me, and in her eyes showed what she was thinking and petrified to say. I continued to tell her what I saw.

"I didn't recognize myself because my skin was dry and discolored. The vibrancy of my natural color had turned gray. I hurried out of the bathroom and headed back over to my dresser, but the picture was gone. Looked everywhere and it was gone," I shuddered.

"When I finally fell asleep, I started to dream of the Café where Jeremy and I had met. The only thing different was that I was standing outside of the Café looking through the window as if I was observing it from a distance. It was like it was yesterday when we met. Everything was so lucid, I stood there and watched as we conversed. As I gazed at the memory of what my life used to be in my dream, I saw a reflection of the same little boy that I saw at the Camelot Hotel that I told you about. He was standing on the sidewalk right behind me. The tone of the dream completely changed when the boy showed up." I paused.

"The times that he would appear, he would just sit and stare at me. When I turned around in the dream, he just stood there. I asked him where his mommy was and all he did was smile and reach out to me. I squatted down to reach out for him, when he walked closer towards me. I was about to pick him up when he whispered in my ear saying 'I'm cold, it's so dark in here!' He ran away from me and vanished around the corner. That is when I woke up. I had actually thought about not going into to work today, but I need to focus my thoughts elsewhere."

"Maybe that is the problem, Michelle. This is something you have admitted you have to face. In a way, you are still running from the decision you made. Let me ask you this, since you felt like he was going to boy, what would you have named him if you kept the baby?" She asked.

With a tremor in my voice, I responded to her saying his name would have been Elijah.

"That would have been a beautiful name for him, Michelle. Are you going to be able to make through your evening tonight at work?"

"Yes, I will be okay. I know I have to face the music and again. I do feel terrible for putting Jeremy before me and the needs of my baby. I know there are consequences that I would have to pay for in regard to the choice I made.

25 Michelle Sullivan- Connected Forever

I walked into work with my heart feeling so heavy with many emotions, I did everything I could to focus on work. That attempt was completely sidetracked, when I saw him step off the elevator heading for the front desk. I was on my way back out to the front desk after grabbing the paperwork, I needed from the back office when Jeremy Stone walked up. After all this, I thought I was never going to see him again, especially after he told me I was not the woman for him.

I mumbled under my breath as he walked towards me, saying "what the hell does he want?"

I know I had this scowled look on my face when he approached me. He spoke hesitantly at first, because he did not know how I was going to respond to him.

"Hello, Michelle. How have you been?"

I couldn't tell him I have been tormented inside, so I put on a brave face and responded saying, "I am doing great. I just have been really focusing on work. How have you been?"

"I have not been doing so well, can we talk do you have a moment?" He asked.

I told my two front desk agents to cover the front

desk, while I stepped away for a moment.

What could he possibly want to talk to me about? I really hope this is not going to be one of those conversations where he is trying to justify his behavior just to see if I have forgiven him. He was such a jack ass during the ending of our relationship. We sat not too far away from the front desk at a booth in the bar, just in case my employees needed me. I sat back and silence and let him speak, while I watched his body language as well. When he began to talk, he automatically started to fidget with his clothes, which I noticed over the time of knowing him that he was fabricating what he was saying. While he was speaking, he had a hard time looking me in my eyes also.

The first thing that came out of him was saying that he was sorry, and how he has been miserable thinking about the way he treated me when I was carrying his child. I wondered why it took him so long to come to me with this, although it was nice to hear whether he meant it or not. I knew I had to forgive for myself and not hold any animosity, this was for me, not for his gratification.

"Jeremy, you can't even look at me while you are speaking. I know you feel guilty about what you did! Whether you mean the apology or not, I have to forgive you for myself, so I won't continue to struggle with what we went through at the end of our relationship. I honestly told myself that I was not going to let you know that over the years I have also been miserable. I don't care that you know, because this is what I need to move on. I do forgive you, so if that is what you came here for, there you have it," I said.

I stood to walk away, when he grabbed my hand, "Michelle, wait."

I turned to look at him and he was staring me back in my face. For a moment, I saw the man I fell in love with.

"Yes, Jeremy? What is it? I have to get back to work."

"I still love you Michelle!"

For a split second, I believed what he was saying until the elevator door dinged and off stepped the woman I saw him in the café with that day. As I pulled my hand away, he stood because he saw her also. Low and behold, her belly clearly showed she was very far into her pregnancy. I had nothing else to say to him, I just looked at him with sheer disappointment and walked away.

There was nothing that she said to me as we crossed paths as I headed back to the front desk and she headed towards him. I went to the back office and started to cry because my own guilt had set in again. For some reason, I felt like it was my fault that he didn't want that life with me. I quickly had to shake that feeling off because I have played that scenario over and over in my mind and I had to realize some things are not to be.

As I sat at my desk, the phone rung and it was Kim calling to check on me.

"Hello! Hey, girl! I was calling to check on you!"

"Hey Kim, you seem to call just when I need you." I laughed.

"Why do you say that, what is going on?" Kim asked.

"You won't believe who walked off of the elevator as I was heading out to the front desk tonight."

"Who? Do you need me to come up there?"

I laughed and said, "no, I'm fine."

"Well, who was it?"

"It was Jeremy," I said.

"What, really after all of this time! What did he want?"

"He said he wanted to talk for a moment. I kind of felt he had come looking for closure just to see if I had forgiven him for how our relationship ended. Of course, he started the conversation with saying he was sorry, but what I noticed was that he began to fidget with his clothes, and he wouldn't even look me in the eye at first. When he would do that when we were in a relationship, I knew he was hiding something. I did let him know that I had forgiven him. But whether or not he was sincere regarding his apology, I didn't care. I was forgiving him for my own well-being. I stood to walk away from him and that's when he grabbed my hand and he told me that he still loved me!"

"Did you believe him?" She asked shocked.

"I did until the woman I saw him in the café with stepped out of the elevator. What made it more bizarre was that she was pregnant!" I said.

"Michelle, you are lying!"

"No, I promise you I am telling you the truth! She was much farther along in her pregnancy than I was. When I saw that I had nothing else to say to him I just snatched my hand away and looked at him like he was the most pathetic person."

"Did you say anything to her?" She asked.

"No, there was need or reason to say anything to her. My mind tried to send me back into that guilt trip as if I did something wrong to the reason why he didn't want me, but I snapped out of it really quick, realizing some things are not meant to be."

"Michelle, are you sure you will be able to make it through your shift tonight?" She asked.

"Yes, I'm going to dive into these reports. I will call you tomorrow. Thank you for checking on me. I love you Kim, and don't ever forget that."

"Aww, girl. You know I love you too!" She said.

Today, for some odd reason, time seemed to be flying at work. The next thing I know, I looked at the clock and it was 3:00 am. I stood there still going over the nightly audits when the music changed to I*n the Arms of an Angel* by Sarah McLachlan. I kind of thought that was strange because the music doesn't change unless an employee does it, and I was the only one that was there.

I went to the back and changed the music back to the approved station. The lobby was quiet as I clicked away on the keyboard only to look up and see a little boy about the age of four sitting on the couch with his back facing the front desk. He was just sitting there staring at the TV in the bar lobby. I thought maybe he beat his mother down the hall and was waiting for her.

I know people lock themselves out of their hotel room all the time and they come to the front desk late into the night wanting a new key. After another 15 minutes had passed, I looked up again only to notice the little boy looking at me. A chill shot through my body as I began to walk from behind the counter, as I got closer to the little boy my heart started to beat rapidly.

How was it possible that he looked just like the little boy from my dream? Despite what I was feeling inside, I sat down next him and touched him on the shoulder. I asked, "Are you okay? Where is your mother? Where did you come from?"

He turned toward me and again said the same thing the little boy said in the dream, "I'm cold, it's so dark in here!"

I slid back away from him; my whole body started to tremble. I asked, "what did you say?"

He responded again to me, but what he said to me this time I knew I would not come back from! I was looking at my child. The child that I aborted. My blessing that was mine. I abused that gift. He came back to get me. How could I live when I have taken his life!

He said, "it's so dark in here. You are my mommy! Why did you leave me here? I have always been with you this whole time watching you, mommy! I want you to come with me!"

Again, his eyes had turned a dark piercing grey just as they did before. He placed his little hand on my chest, and I felt everything that he experienced. I slowly began to feel the life being sapped out of my body. It was hard for me to breathe. My chest had begun to have this burning sensation. I felt the crushing pressure all over my body. I was unable to move my body, it had become debilitated. My thoughts were burning me from the inside out.

What did I do to deserve to see the child I was supposed to have? What did I do to deserve to hear his voice? See him smile, touch his skin. I did not deserve any of it, it was my punishment to relive what I put him through. I never would have thought just because he was still a miracle inside of me that he would not feel the pain from my actions. Feeling lifeless as his hand remained placed on my chest, the tears poured down my face as I struggled to say, "I am sorry... momma is so sorry, baby."

He removed his hand. This was my child looking back at me and I didn't want to believe anything else, I wanted to hold onto him as long as possible, however long that would be. As I held him, he said, "come with me mommy."

"Where are we going sweetie?" I asked.

"I won't be cold anymore if you come with me. Here take my hand mommy. Tears continued to roll down my face as I took his hand. I instantly felt cold. I walked with him down the hall, letting him lead the way. I felt like I was in a half-conscious state of mind.

It was said that when my employees returned, they saw me walking down the hallway, looking as if I was holding someone's hand. They called out my name, but I didn't respond. When I reached the last elevator on the left, I looked down the hallway in their direction and just stepped into elevator. He pushed the button to the 33rd floor. When he did, I knew exactly what it referenced to. I was at peace with what was waiting for me. I had closure. The number 33 has a significant meaning that resonates with the energies of compassion, blessings, inspiration, honesty, discipline, bravery and courage. The number 33 tells us that 'all things are possible'. 33 is also the number that symbolizes 'guidance'. In this, my child was my blessing. A gift I did not value and I was disciplined over the years for the decision I made to destroy a life, which I did not have the right to do! Now with bravery and courage, I walk with him into that dark place where he has been cold and alone.

When the doors opened, I don't know what I expected to see. But, it was pitch black, wet, and cold. An unseen force had seemed to be guiding me, as I proceeded to step forward. I knew I had accepted my destiny. I was no longer afraid. I let go of his hand and picked him up, holding him so tight. This is my child and mommy has come with you to keep you warm, no more darkness baby! The surrounding area changed into light.

CPSIA information can be obtained
at www.ICGtesting.com
Printed in the USA
LVHW042047230421
685384LV00002B/104

Contents

Common medical problems that occur in the aging
population and their mode of presentation in the
dental office are reviewed. These problems can be
sensory, motor, metabolic, or emotional. Common
features are multiplicity and chronicity. There are
specific difficulties in both the ambulatory and
inpatient setting which must be considered in the
patient-doctor relationship.

In senescence there is a decrease both in the diameter
and the number of muscle fibers. The chief
concomitants of this diminution are an increase in
fat content and the deposition of the "aging pigment"
lipofuscin. At the cellular molecular level actomyosin
ATPase and creatine phosphokinase specific activities
also decline with age and with age-related declining
function.

Cementum remains metabolically and proliferatively
low-keyed, but viable and formative throughout life.
It should remain responsive to surgical intervention
and other stresses in the aged.